The Alchemist's Mistress

The Alchemist's Mistress   by Mol Smith

He took her from the streets of Victorian
London and made her his own

by Mol Smith

ONVIEW BOOKS
The Alchemist's Mistress
by Mol Smith

Published by Onview.net Ltd
2025

Onview.net Ltd. Registered Office:
23 Segsbury Road, Wantage,
Oxfordshire. OX12 9XP
www.onview.net

The moral right of the author has been asserted.
This book is dedicated to Alan Edgar Poe 1809-1849 and Bram
Stoker 1847-1912.

First Published 2025 by (Onview Books) Onview.net Ltd.
ISBN: 978-1-9192041-0-9
Imprint: Independently published[1]

Contents

Introduction

I write very fast, sometimes producing a book once a month. They always centre around several topics. I guess they contain a lot of sexual activity or desire of such by the characters. I believe the sexual urge underpins, invisibly, nearly all of human activity.

Like animals, nature has made us to grow to adulthood, mate, have offspring and mind them until they can mind themselves. And then we perish. The primaeval emotion which drives this is from the most primitive part of our brain. It often comes into conflict with our higher thoughts, and creates a quest for power in many, so they can secure good partners to mate with.

The other topic I use is contact and entanglement with processes or events outside of the characters' control. I like to surprise my readers, and myself.

I start each story with a single premise and other than the original setting, I have no story plan, plot or ending worked out. I set the stage, put my characters upon it, and then let them loose. They write the story with their antics and acts, their entanglement with each other—their desires, addictions, triumphs and failings, forming the plot, and providing me with a fly on the wall view of all this.

I am the close observer writing about them.

If you visit my website at *molsmith.org.uk* you will discover short, video film, tie-ins to this book.

In this work, I've deliberately coaxed my characters to vie against and encounter their primaeval sexual motivations against a background of ever-changing discovery. In many ways, it's an exaggeration, or possibly—a parody of our lives, if you look deep enough behind the scenes. Enjoy!

This work has not been subjected to professional editing which leaves it vulnerable to typos and errors. I apologise. I thought it too extreme for my normal editors to correct.

Mol
July 2025

A Lady In Rags

Chapter 1: A Lady In Rags

Fog had settled over the East End in a low, sour breath, the kind that slicked the cobbles and soaked the wool of the poor until it stank worse than the sheep it had been sheared and stolen from. She sat with her back to a brick wall, knees drawn up, fingers cramped into fists inside a man's cut-down gloves. A gift from a toff to a beggar, thinking he could buy sexual favours with his meagre offerings. She had run off clutching them. When was that? One night or twenty ago?

She had no name to put against the cold or the hunger. When she tried, it was as if she leaned over a well with no bottom and her voice fell, fell, and never struck. Only sounds remained: a violin waltz, the hiss of gas, laughter in a room of mirrors; and—worse—the quiet instruction of a man's voice close to her ear: drink.

Boots went past. A pair, then three. A shout further down, a scuffle. She tipped her head to keep watch from the corner of her eye. Men who looked too long at a woman who looked too poor. A cart wheel complained as it struck a rut. Somewhere a kettle lid clattered and a child cried and no one minded. She gathered herself smaller against the wall, a broken-winged bird trapped near the gutter in the rain.

"Miss?"

The voice came from the fog as if someone had opened a door onto a different room. Not the bark of a watchman, not the careless slur of a drunk; polite, precise, a tone that assumed an answer would be given because it always was.

She lifted her head. The man held a lantern low and turned the shield with thumb and forefinger so the light did not dash into her eyes. He wore a dark greatcoat, dry as if the fog respected its boundaries, and a hat with a narrow brim pressed into a firm line above his brow. Clean, that was the first certainty. The second was that he had a habit of looking without staring; his gaze touched and moved on like a physician's hand.

"Are you injured?" he asked.

She thought to say no. The word came as far as her teeth and broke. It was not pain so much as a general crack in her: her feet raw, her shoulders aching from a coat too heavy and too stolen, her head full of a roar when she stood.

"I—" The sound rasped. To her surprise, her hands rose, the way a child's might when a parent returned from an ordinary day.

He set the lantern on the cobbles. "Forgive me," he said, "I am Dr Sebastian Veyl. May I take your pulse?"

She nodded, then frowned at herself for nodding, and then it did not matter because he had taken one of her fists gently in his gloved hand and prised the fingers open. His glove slid off with a practised tug; his skin was warm. He did not count aloud. His expression barely altered, save for a quick readjustment of the mouth, as if he filed the number away. He released her hands.

"You're chilled and thirsty," he said, as if informing her of the weather. "And you haven't eaten since yesterday. There's a carriage half a street over. If you would allow me, I'll bring you somewhere warm."

She watched his face and then the lantern and then the fog. Men who lifted poor girls into carriages did not usually ask permission. They did not keep their voices quiet to avoid frightening them. She listened for the other sounds—the rustle of accomplices, the click of a watchman's cane—but there was nothing except the sigh of the wet night.

"Where?" she managed.

"My house," he said. "Belgravia."

She almost laughed at that, the word outrageous in the damp. "I'm not a whore. We could go to the police instead," she said, surprising herself. It took effort not to whisper.

"We can," he agreed, without a pause. "We may, if you prefer. I warn you: they'll be brisk with you, and offer bread. I'll be slower, and offer soup, and shelter. If I alarm you at any point, you can step out. Do you think you can stand?"

There it was again, the assumption of choice spoken as if it were natural to her. She pushed herself up and the alley wavered. The world tilted to the left and then was caught by his hand under her elbow. He smelled of soap and something metal, bitter and clean.

"Slowly," he said. "There. We'll go now."

He did not lift her so much as direct her weight until walking became possible. Two turns took them out of the black slit of the alley and into a street not much better, except that the lamps here were properly fed and the buildings had the decency not to lean. He knocked on the side of a closed door with the lantern handle; an answer came immediately, and a man in a coachman's coat appeared and touched the brim of his hat.

"Home," Dr Veyl said. "As quick as is bearable."

The interior of the carriage was a little room with red velvet seats and a faint perfume of oil and leather. She sat on the edge, hands flat on her knees, ready to fly. Dr Veyl settled opposite her and hung the lantern so that it cast a pool of light between them.

"Do you know your name?" he asked, not unkindly.

She had tried to knit one out of scraps these last days—Ellen, Emilie, a syllable that began with C and broke, a surname that tasted of chalk. It would not hold.

"No," she said.

"Do you know a direction? A district? Anyone you trust? A forgotten home?"

She shook her head. The motion threatened the carriage to rock.

He considered her for a moment in a way that did not feel like being measured for sale. "Very well," he said. "I shall lend you one of mine, until you find it. We shall call you 'Miss Merton' at the door— for the sake of the servants, you understand? They don't like persons without names."

She tried the word in her mouth—Merton—felt the shape of it. It struck something far away and the ripple came back empty.

"Do you do this often?" she asked. "Collect stray cats?," and she meant it to sound rude, but it came out near to being grateful.

"No," he said. "Only when I am on my way home from a lecture on the specific heat to melt tin, and when the evening has been otherwise unremarkable."

She looked from his face to the window and the fog beyond. "Tin," she repeated, as if testing a coin.

"Metals are sometimes less inert than we like to think," he said, as if that were a joke between them. "Forgive me. You see cold and I see properties."

The carriage jolted. She gripped the strap. The strap was cleaner than anything her hands had held in weeks; it conjured images in her touch—a history, it's slaughter on a day when the farmer, so kind to feed her, gave the dry cow a the promise of a day out from the grassless field.

They made their way west by streets that widened and grew quieter, until the fog seemed to grow shy of following. When the carriage at last stopped, the world outside the window held more light and less muck; the steps were marble and the knocker on the door had a lion for a face. The servant who answered their ring took in her state with a flicker in the eyes and then folded his expression smooth.

"Miss Merton," Dr Veyl said, and they moved inside as if the entrance hall had been expecting them.

Warmth did not so much strike her, as seep. The tiles shone, black and cream, and the air carried a flavour of beeswax and something additional, faint as an aftertaste. A woman came forward from a side door, brisk, grey-haired, with a mouth that remembered smiling and a brow that could not afford it.

"Maggie," Dr Veyl said, "We shall have broth, and the lavender bath warmed. Miss Merton, our guest, has been overset. I will have no talk, now or later, of the East End. Her present circumstances are not our concern."

"Aye, sir," Maggie said, and dipped her head to the girl in a gesture that was almost a curtsy, and nearly kind. But also an obeyance of his wishes.

"Will you come?" she asked, to the girl, not the doctor. "You look as if you might fall to dust if I blow. I'll not blow. I'll carry, if you like."

"I can walk," the girl said, though her legs were treacherous. She followed Maggie up a staircase that did not creak. The banister shone like a river at night. On the landing, a tall mirror reflected a poor copy of herself—too thin, clothes hanging, hair hacked ragged—but the face under the dirt struck her as a sketch of something elegant that had gone wrong. Her eyes looked older than her skin.

The room Maggie opened for her was not a room she had earned. The bed had a canopy, clean sheets, and was covered with thick warm blankets. The fire had been made ready but not yet lit. A porcelain pitcher steamed faintly on the washstand. A tin bath to one side, steamed the same, as if the room had expected her.

"I've set out the bath," Maggie said. "There's soap that doesn't catch. I'm to fetch broth. If you'll let me take your things." She glanced at the coat, the ruined boots. "Or I can burn the lot, and you may start clean."

"Burn them," she said, surprising herself with how quickly the words came. The clothes felt not just filthy but unlucky.

Maggie nodded once, businesslike, and took the bundle with two hands. "Water first," she said over her shoulder. "There's peppermint in the cabinet for the belly. If your head swims, sit. Don't be brave; it doesn't pay."

When the door closed, silence gathered differently than it had in the alley. She stood for a moment with her hands at her sides, as if awaiting orders from her own body, and then moved. The bath took her to the hips, then the ribs, then the throat, and she sank as a stone does, with relief. The heat stung, then soothed. She worked at the grime until a face emerged. The bones were fine: cheek and brow and jaw set all suggested a careful house, good food, somebody who had said no to her only for sport. She flinched away from the thought as if it were a light too bright for her present eyes.

When Maggie returned with the tray, she found the girl seated, hair wrapped in a towel, skin raised in gooseflesh from the bath.

The broth steamed, and the spoonful she took scalded her tongue so that tears sprang without her consent. She ate anyway until her hands steadied.

"Good," Maggie said. "Follow me."

She took her to another, larger bedroom, all made ready, with sheets and blankets cornered back, and an oil lamp glowing on a walnut -finished bedside table. A writing desk lay beneath a curtained window.

She studied the girl in a way different from Dr Veyl's—less measuring, more worrying about where to tuck blankets.

"What am I to call you?" the girl asked.

"Maggie Rooke," she said. "Housekeeper. Nurse if needs must. Wallet if the house goes poorer for a week. Friend, if you push me."

"I will try not to push," the girl said.

Maggie glanced at the door and lowered her voice. "The doctor is..." She searched for a word and settled for obedient. "He likes things in order. He keeps to his purposes. That's a blessing if you're ill. It's a nuisance if you're not. Don't cross him for sport. And don't sign your name to anything at night."

The girl frowned. "I don't have a name to sign."

"Then all the more reason not to borrow one in the dark," Maggie said. "Sleep. That's what will save you first, not soup and not orders. I'll be outside, downstairs, if you stir. Just go to the door and call for me."

When Maggie left, the room shifted from someone's workplace and bedroom, to a place she might temporarily inhabit. She slid under the sheets with the guilty thrill of a thief in a silk shop. The pillow took the weight of her head as if it had been cast for it. Her eyes closed.

At once, she was not in the room.

She was in a hall that smelled of beeswax and lemons, but brighter than this one, brighter than any hall she could remember being in; and there were a hundred lights from large candles on a hundred arms and the lights made a river along the ceiling. Music turned, one two three, a the pulse of a Vienna waltz, and she was turning with it, the hem of her gown a pale cloud. She glanced up, and there was a mask higher than hers, a man's chin below the silver, a mouth that smiled in a way that asked permission and did not wait for it. They were alone in the centre of the room, though the room was crowded; the crowd was a ring of ghosts from the throat down. Laughter touched her cheek like a hand. She was thirsty. The man bent and said something into her ear, something close and reasonable: drink.

A glass reached her mouth. The rim was cold. The liquid was a sting and then sweetness and then metal sliding onto her tongue like a coin under the skin. She swallowed and lights bent. The ceiling tipped; the faces tilted; the river of light ran downhill very fast and she went with it. The last thing she saw before the dark was a gloved hand closing a small, polished lid over the candle flame.

She gasped herself awake, fingers clawing at the counterpane. The room returned with a jump: coals banked in the grate, the faint murmur of the house as if its timbers talked. She pressed her palm against her sternum until her heart learned the tempo of now and not that of a runner, trying to escape menace.

She lay awhile, listening. A carriage rolled by outside, slow. Pipes ticked in the wall as if water were changing its mind. From somewhere lower, where rooms were ordered for work rather than comfort, a brief metallic clink sounded and then ceased, as if a piece of glass had touched another and then thought better of focusing on it.

She ought to sleep again. Instead, she got up and crossed to the dressing table where someone had set out a brush and a comb, a small bottle of lamp oil, a square of folded linen as crisp as a book. A locket lay there, not hers, oval, silver, blank of stone or engraving. The chain slid over her fingers like a thought being agreed with. She opened it. There was no miniature inside, only a small hollow and, curiously, the faintest scent, not of perfume but of—she could not name it— something clean and not quite clean, a winter's breath on a coin. Momentarily, did she see a picture inside?, No. It was empty.

She closed it. The hinge made a small, accurate sound, like a decision. The sound of a total seal, like that of a tomb crafted by the finest carpenter.

A knock at the door, soft. She started, and the locket slipped and tapped onto the table. "Yes?" she said.

The door opened far enough to admit a slice of light and the man who had rescued her. He had removed his hat; his hair was more grey than black and arranged itself in a way that suggested it had tried to curl and been discouraged. He carried a small case in his left hand. In his right, between finger and thumb, with a delicate surgeon's steadiness, he held a glass dropper. The bulb was of dark rubber, the tube thin as a willow switch. At its tip, a single bead of liquid hung, catching the lamplight and holding it—gold, not yellow, something richer and warmer that made the spot where it touched air look gilded.

"I am sorry to disturb you," Dr Veyl said in the tone of a man who has checked his reasons and found them sufficient. "I know the day has been an affront. Sleep will do most of the work; the remainder…" He looked at the drop poised between them and then at her face. "This will persuade your nerves to lay down their arms."

She watched the bead gather enough weight to loosen but not fall. The smell reached her then, faint, and familiar and unplaceable, like the name at the edge of a tongue. Metal. Warmth. Something that was not quite a taste and not quite a memory.

"What is it?" she asked.

"An old friend in a new suit," he said. "A restorative. One drop and the noise and fractured thoughts will recede. You'll keep your wits; you will simply not hear them argue for a while."

He did not step further without her invitation. The strange courtesy of it made her chest ache.

"Will I dream?" she asked, surprising herself with the question.

"Yes," he said, and something in his mouth altered; a smile that was not unkind and not entirely reassuring. "But you will be able to wake when you wish."

She looked at the drop again, how it had made a tiny lens of the room around it. She thought of fog and hunger and a voice telling her to drink; of Maggie's plain kindness; of the portrait-hall in her dream and the river of light. She thought of the way everyone in the carriage and then in this house had called her by a name and how the name had not refused them. She was very tired of wrestling the day by herself.

"Very well," she said. Her voice was steady. "Only—tell me first what I am to be called tomorrow."

He considered that, as if the order of it mattered. "Clara," he said at last. "Clara Merton. It will do until you choose otherwise."

"Clara," she tried. It did not fall all the way down the well. It struck somewhere and sent back a faint, shocked answering note.

He came to the bedside. The lamp threw his profile clear: the unmoved mouth, the eyes that told the truth and something besides. He lifted the dropper slightly.

"Open your mouth," Dr Veyl said, almost gently. "For your nerves."

Clara parted her lips. The drop slid from the glass like a bead of sun and touched the tip of her tongue before she could brace herself. It burst against her palate—no taste at first, only a coolness like a winter's breath. Then a thread of sweetness unspooled through her mouth, warm as honey, but without weight, followed by a faint metallic whisper, as if a coin of the purest gold had melted into vapour.

It was not the blunt rush of brandy or the dizzy pinch of laudanum. The effect spread with deliberation, as though the liquid knew its path and had walked it before. Her heartbeat slowed to a comfortable thud. The ache in her calves unwound. The tight clutch in her chest dissolved until it was only a shadow of itself. The room seemed to stand closer to her, the colours deepening—the black of the counterpane rich as ink, the gold braid on Veyl's cuff catching light like a star seen through water.

"There now," he said, withdrawing the dropper. "Your nerves will behave. Rest is all that is required of you."

She swallowed, found her voice. "It… tastes familiar."

"It would," Veyl replied with a slight, unreadable tilt of the mouth. "Memory runs deeper than mind." He placed something on the dressing table as if placing a clock where she might consult it.

He paused at the door. "If you dream of troubling things, remind yourself they are only guests. You may send them away."

And he was gone, as soundlessly as he had entered.

Alone again, Clara sat for a long moment on the bed's edge, the lamp's light coiling in the glass dropper still on the table. Her fingers twitched with the urge to touch it, to confirm the bead was gone. The strange calm settled deeper—not drowsiness, exactly, but the sensation of having been tuned, like an instrument brought into key.

She slid under the counterpane and closed her eyes.

The dream began without preamble. She was standing in a gallery of tall, narrow mirrors. Each reflected her in different light—one dressed in rags, another in a gown stitched from moonlight, another with hair swept into a style she had never worn but knew had once been hers. Footsteps sounded behind her, slow and assured. She turned, expecting the silver mask from before.

It was Dr Veyl.

Not quite as he had looked in the lamplight upstairs—younger, though the hair still silvered; taller, perhaps, or simply filling the space with more ease. He offered his hand, palm upward, as though inviting her to dance. She placed hers in it without hesitation.

"You're feeling better," he said. It was not a question.

"Yes," she answered, and knew she was speaking the truth.

He led her past the mirrors. In each, the versions of herself turned their heads to follow, their eyes bright as if urging her onward.

"Why am I here?" she asked.

"To see yourself clearly," he said. "Few are given the chance."

They came to a mirror unlike the others: a single pane of glass so clear it might have been air, framed in polished brass. In it, Clara saw no reflection at all—only a faint shimmer, as though something were waiting to step forward if she leaned close enough.

She did. The shimmer parted like mist, and she glimpsed a figure within—herself again, but with eyes that caught the light like molten gold.

She woke with a start, heart quickened. The calm of the elixir still wrapped her like a second skin, but the image lingered, stubborn as a stain on glass.

A faint tapping drew her attention to the window. She crossed the room and looked out. The fog had lifted just enough to reveal the dark outline of the garden wall and the street beyond. The tap came again—a bare branch in the wind, nothing more. Still, she thought she saw movement near the corner of the wall: the shape of a man's coat, dissolving into shadow.

When she turned back toward the bed, the silver locket lay open on the dressing table.

The First Morning

Chapter 2: The First Morning

When she woke, the light in the room had the buttery quality of a winter morning in the city, filtered through gauze curtains and the faint smoke of chimneys. For a moment, she thought she had dreamt the night before: the fog, the carriage, the bath, the locket, the bead of gold. But her body knew better. Her limbs were unknotted, her head clear in a way that seemed almost theatrical, as if someone had staged the sensation for her benefit.

Maggie came in without knocking, a tray balanced in her hands. Tea steamed in the pot; the scent of warm bread filled the space between them.

"Well," Maggie said, setting the tray on the low table, "You look less like death's errand girl today."

Clara drew the bed covering down to her waist and sat up. "I feel… strange," she said. "Not unwell, only… very certain that I am awake."

Maggie's eyes narrowed briefly, but she said nothing about it. "Tea before you faint, if you please. The master's gone out. You're to eat and rest. No roaming."

Clara poured herself a cup. The China was thin enough to tremble under her fingers, yet the tea did not slosh. She realised her hands were utterly steady. "Why am I here, Maggie?"

The woman looked towards the bedroom door and back at her. "Because the master wishes you here." Her face turned briefly to a warning and then a strained smile as she turned and left.

After breakfast, she dressed in the plain gown laid out for her—not new, but good cloth, soft from washing. In the tall mirror by the wardrobe, she paused. Her face seemed subtly altered: no change in the shape of it, but in the way the light acknowledged her cheekbones, the depth of her gaze. She leaned closer. The pupils were wider than they ought to be in morning light, catching more than they gave back.

She thought of the gold bead on her tongue. The memory was almost pleasant.

The rest of the house was awake in a quiet way. Somewhere below, a clock chimed nine. In the long hallway, dust motes shifted like lazy sparks. She trailed her hand along the wall's panelling as she explored the wood, as if it held heat from another source entirely. The hall was short and led to the stairs.

In the morning room, she found Maggie at a writing desk, sealing a letter with a wax stamp. Maggie looked up, startled, as though she had not expected to be seen.

"Was I not meant to come down?" Clara asked.

"You were," Maggie said too quickly, "but it's cold in here. Sit closer to the fire if you're set on staying."

Clara took a seat. The front door opened and closed. Dr Veyl's voice, low and even, carried from the hall as he removed his gloves and coat. When he entered, the air seemed to adjust itself. Maggie rose immediately, smoothing her apron.

"Miss Merton," he said, as though the name had always belonged to her. "I see the colour has returned."

She inclined her head. "I slept well."

"I expected you would." He took a chair opposite her, one gloved hand resting on his knee. "The mind repairs itself most efficiently when the body is at ease. In some, the effect is more pronounced than in others."

Clara wondered whether he was speaking of the elixir or of herself. "And which am I?" she asked lightly.

His mouth curved. "Promising."

The word sat in the air between them like a coin on a scale, its weight to be decided later.

Veyl's gaze shifted briefly to Maggie, who was still standing at her post.

"That will be all for now," he said.

When the door had closed behind her, Clara leaned forward slightly. "May I ask you something?"

"You may."

"What was in the drop you gave me?"

"A compound of my own design. Entirely benign, I assure you. A modern refinement of an ancient restorative medicine. Older than either of us. I could explain its workings in terms of chemical reaction, but the result would be the same—you feel better today than yesterday."

"And tomorrow?"

"That will depend," he said. "On you."

A carriage rattled past outside, drawing her attention to the window. In the pale light, she caught the briefest movement beyond the iron gate: the same dark coat she had thought she saw last night by the garden wall. It vanished into the flow of the street before she could decide whether to mention it.

Veyl followed her glance. "The street is busy this time of day," he said easily. "People pass."

"Yes," she said. But her mind had caught on something else—the faintest aftertaste of metal that still lingered, as if the drop had marked her on the inside.

She began to wonder then, why would this wealthy gentleman rescue her from the gutters of London? Did not rich men come often at night, under cover of darkness, to prey with their sexual wildness, on the weak women, stealing them away to be used and discarded, like the buckets of shit on the streets, emptied on the morning carts.

"Why did you really bring me here?"

He looked at her with a playfulness in his eyes. Did she not just notice will-o'-the-wisps darting with lanterns across his dark pupils?

"I thought I needed a student, and someone who might be desperate enough to listen."

"Not kindness and the boredom of the melting temperature of tin, them."

He smiled with delight, "There, a talent. You have an excellent memory."

"Ha. Short term. I am absent from any time before the streets." She said.

"As may be. Best to focus on the now and the future. The past, all past, already died a second ago."

He stood up and said, "Come with me, please." As they walked the corridors and climbed flights of stairs, he spoke to her in silken words that refused to bounce harshly from the wooden panelled walls. It was as though he spoke not of ordinary things, but of secrets too powerful for the house not to suffocate at birth, lest they drew breath outside and spread like seeds on the wind.

They arrived outside a large oak door. Clara stared at the faces that seemed to laugh, stare, and cry on the panels, their grain forming drawings in the mind.

"Maggie took you to the overnight guest room to sleep last night. Rightly, she thought you too weak for so many flights of stairs. I have work to do, but I'll come and fetch you in an hour or so. But first, I wished to bring you to a bedroom of your own if you care to stay with us."

Am I to be his plaything? Not one night of rape and thrown away or back into the gutter?

He took a step back and gestured with his hand, indicating to her to open the door. She put her hand on the brass knob with the delicate touch of a mouse first entering a trap that will break its neck, as sure as it was true its little nose would only smell the feast it would never savour.

As he saw her hesitation, he said, "There are fine clothes in the wardrobes, pen, paper, a writing desk...." adding a feast to the scrap on the spike at the end of the wood with the spring poised above it, "...books, a view from high up over Belgravia; shoes, a feathered bed, washing bowl, scents, all the thing you might find a comfort to you." Her hand was lured further, and she slowly twisted the knob.

She stopped, removed her hand from the enticing metal that shone with promises too great. Instead, she turned and said, "Why?"

As he replied, he bent forward with an arm extended that twisted the knob and pushed open the heavy door with the merest of movements, as though he had puffed on it to conjure up a magical vista, too beautiful for her eyes and mind to resist, as he said. "I need an apprentice."

She stood there like a bauble beside a diamond until her foot moved without her agreement and carried her in.

"Enjoy exploring. I'll return later."

He closed the door behind her. She listened like a bat, but there was no click of a lock being closed. She was there freely, not trapped. She saw her reflection in the long mirror that adorned the wall opposite, and it showed not her that stood there, but a memory of herself as she readied herself for a ball.

She shook it away and went to the wardrobe, opened it, and saw clothes of silk and fineness. Was she dreaming? Had that golden drop put her into a coma, and she is still not awake. She went to the windows, drew back the drapes, and flung them open. Sunlight lit the room in the brightness of warmth that seemed to hang over this area, as though the rich inhabitants of this borough had a sun-magnet buried in the earth here that pulled the rays away from the foggy, dim and damp hovels of the East End, so they could steal it away for their elitist selves.

Unable to restrain herself, she went back to the wardrobe, threw a beautiful dress onto the bed, and began to undress. She caught herself naked in the mirror and went up closer to look at herself. It had been a time since she had seen her own reflection so clearly.

A whisperer in her head began to utter silken words of seduction. Her hands stroked over her breasts, felt their firmness, the hard, erect nipples. She pinched them lightly, the way God must have pinched her there to say, "You're finished, my exquisite creation, as near as perfect as I could make you."

She smiled at her own clever thought, and caught her breath as she saw her hand moving, as though it were stringed like a puppet's hand, to someone else's control stick. The sensations came fast, overwhelming her senses as she let out a gasp and nearly fainted with the shock of ecstasy and bliss, so long now forgotten.

A sound, a faint, muted echo. Did the room just moan with her? An instinct, a flash in her mind, a glint of sun from metal. She spun around towards the open windows, but it wasn't that. It was the locket on the dressing room table. It had caught the sun and thrown a golden ball into the edge of her eye.

It lay innocently enough, but the way it caught the light made it seem to breathe. She crossed the room, her bare feet silent against the thick carpet, and took it in her hand. It was warm—not from the sunbeam, she thought, but as if it had been held moments before. She glanced at the door. Still closed. Still no sound in the corridor

She ran her thumb along the filigree pattern, noticing that the tiny swirls of gold were not purely decorative—they formed a series of interlocking symbols. She pressed the catch.

The hinge whispered open.

Inside, the miniature portrait of a young woman stared back at her. The face was almost her own—slightly fuller cheeks, a different set to the lips, but the same pale skin, the same depth of eyes. She felt a jolt in her chest, a sensation not quite shock and not quite recognition, but an uncomfortable marriage of both.

Under the portrait, pressed so thin it seemed woven into the metal, was a curl of hair the colour of midnight-blue. She touched it with the tip of her nail and felt a faint shiver pass up her arm, as though the hair were part of something still living, or something from a forgotten grave that wanted to root itself again on the surface and in the light.

The air in the room had grown warmer. Or perhaps her skin had. She turned back to the wardrobe and let the dress she had chosen slide from the bed to the floor. Another caught her eye—emerald green, its fabric soft as breath, its cut designed to embrace the waist and fall in a spill of opulent folds. She held it against her body and stepped before the mirror again.

This time, the reflection did not seem content to follow her movements. Her mirrored self-tilted its head a fraction before she did, a languid, deliberate grace. The corner of its mouth lifted in a smile that did not quite reach the eyes. She dropped the dress. Her pulse began to quicken—not in fear exactly, but in a kind of alertness, a sharpening of senses as though the air had become charged with a coming storm.

A knock at the door—light, measured, no urgency.

"Yes?" she called.

Maggie stepped in, her expression carefully neutral, though her eyes darted at once to Clara's undressed state before returning to her face as impassive observers. Did Clara sense a second of envy in her face, or a delicate lust, before the polite smile drew the cloak across to hide it?

"Master Veyl says he will see you in the study," she said.

Clara lifted her chin. "And if I choose not to?"

Maggie hesitated, then said, "He told me to say… you might find it instructive."

"Instructive," Clara repeated.

"Yes, miss. His words exactly."

"Maggie stepped back into the hall, leaving the door ajar.

Clara dressed—not in the plain gown laid out for her that morning, but in the emerald dress, now discarded by the foot of the bed. It clung in ways she did not expect, whispering against her skin as she moved. It felt like fingers of a glove stuffed with cotton wool, lightly fondling them. She liked it, found it pleasing as though the dress longed to make love to her. When she reached the door, she paused, glancing once more back at the mirror. The reflection was as it should be this time, obedient and exact. But as she turned away, she thought—just for an instant—that it lingered a heartbeat longer before following.

The corridor beyond was much dimmer than her bedroom. The light filtered through stained glass panels that turned the air into fractured shards of amber and crimson. Her bare hand brushed the banister as she descended the first short flight of stairs. The wood felt warm, as though it had recently been touched—or gripped—by many others before her.

The house had that curious stillness peculiar to large London homes in the day, when the street beyond was bustling, but the rooms themselves seemed to dream. A clock ticked somewhere in the distance, its beat like a steady heart, slow and deliberate. They descended another and longer flight of stairs. Clara saw familiarity, the hall to the entrance. She stopped to check her bearings.

"This way. One more flight," Maggie said, waiting halfway down the next hall, standing beside a door she had never seen opened before.

Maggie went through and she followed, down a spiralling staircase with none of the splendour of the house; wrought iron sides and handrail, metal steps, poor gas lighting.

Maggie waited at the bottom as she stepped off the last metal plate. They stood before a metal door, like the type which might be found guarding a vault full of gold bars. She offered Clara a brief nod, knocked once, and pushed the door just far enough for Clara to step through. Then she retreated without a word, the sound of her shoes clattering up the metal staircase in haste and quickly fading to nothing.

The first thing Clara noticed was the smell—an unfamiliar mingling of beeswax, coal smoke, and something sharper, metallic yet sweet, like a fruit just on the verge of spoiling. Several tall lamps burned, their glow catching on the brass and glass of scientific instruments arrayed along the walls and tables.

A tall bookcase stood open, its shelves not filled with books but with glass vessels—flasks of liquid that shimmered in hues too vivid for nature, powders that seemed to move within their containers as if stirred by an unseen breeze. Above the mantelpiece hung a large, circular diagram drawn in gold and black ink on aged parchment: an intricate wheel of symbols, intersecting circles, and lines that reminded her faintly of astrological charts.

Veyl was at the far table, his sleeves rolled to the elbow, hands steady as he poured a thin thread of liquid from one vessel into another. He did not look up at once.

"Close the door, if you please," he said.

She obeyed, the latch clicking shut behind her.

Only then did he turn. His gaze travelled from her face to the emerald dress and back again, pausing just long enough to acknowledge her choice.

"That colour suits you," he said. "It draws the eye to precisely the right places."

"Your servant said you wished to instruct me," she replied, letting the formality balance the quickening of her pulse.

"I do." He gestured to a tall-backed chair on the other side of the table. "But understand—true instruction is never only a matter of words. It's experience, observation, and the willingness to see patterns where others see only chaos."

She sat, the fabric of the gown whispering against the chair's leather.

He picked up a small crystal vial. The liquid within was pale gold, much like the drop he had given her the night before, but brighter, almost luminescent under the lamp. He held it between two fingers so that the light refracted across her face.

"Alchemy," he began, "is the art of transformation. Metals into gold, the base into the pure. But that is only the child's version of the tale. The true work—the Great Work—concerns not metals, but the essence of life itself. To refine it. To concentrate it. To render it incorruptible."

"I thought that doctrine was a thing of the past, now dying, replaced by chemistry and science," she said.

He looked up suddenly, his attention transferred one hundred percent to her, "You have learning in you, schooling it seems, to a high standard."

He set the vial down before her. The glass was cool to her fingertips, yet the liquid inside seemed to pulse faintly, as though alive.

"And you, therefore, as instinctively thought like a voice screaming out of the mist of time in the London smog at me," he said softly, "have the quality that makes you... ideal."

Clara's throat tightened. "Ideal for what?"

His smile deepened, but his eyes did not. "To learn. To assist. To be far more than you were when I found you."

He moved behind her chair then, close enough that she felt the faint warmth of his presence. "There are three stages to any transformation," he murmured. "The breaking down of what is..." His hands fell to her shoulders... "the purifying of what remains..." were his fingers crawling forward and down towards her breasts, like snakes silently approaching their prey, "...and the shaping of what will be. You have completed the first, though not of your own choice. The breaking down, such that nothing of your former self remains, just the material you were formed to be. The second transformation has begun."

His hand lifted away, hovered close to her, not touching her, but near enough that the air between them seemed charged. "Will you see it through?"

Clara's answer caught in her chest. She thought of the locket, the mirror, the almost-recognition in the portrait. Of the bead of gold that had made the world sharper, richer, and somehow less trustworthy.

"Yes," she said at last, though whether it was her own voice or something the room itself had coaxed from her, or his finger inches from her neck, unseen, but creating a tingling sensation on her nape— she could not tell.

Veyl reached past her for a small glass sphere mounted in a brass stand. Within it, a dark liquid coiled lazily, like smoke trapped in water. He lifted the globe and set it on the table between them.

"This," he said, "is a test of perception. I've given it to many over the years, and most fail."

He rotated the stand so the sphere caught the lamplight. The liquid within began to swirl of its own accord, slow at first, then gathering speed. Threads of silver bled into the darkness, spiralling toward the centre until they formed a single, glimmering point.

"Keep your eyes on that point," he murmured.

Clara did. The point grew brighter until it seemed the rest of the sphere fell away, leaving only that luminous heart. She felt her breath slow, her awareness narrowing to the circle before her. Within the light, something began to take shape—a fragment of a face. Not Veyl's, nor hers, but someone else's entirely. The mouth moved, forming words she could almost hear, as if they were spoken from behind glass.

"What is it?" she whispered.

Veyl's voice came from very far away. "The residue of what once was. A trace. Memory made visible."

The silver point shivered. She felt a sudden deep coldness in her stomach and a release of something; her bladder had opened briefly, then closed. She felt the dampness as the light bled back into the swirling dark, and the image was gone.

She blinked, realising she had been leaning forward, her fingertips nearly touching the glass.

He took the sphere away. "You saw something."

"Yes." Her voice sounded uncertain in her own ears. "A... f... face."

"That's enough for today." He quickly took the sphere away and replaced it on a high shelf. "Not all visions are meant to be understood at once."

She wanted to ask whose face it was, but something in his manner—almost protective, almost possessive—kept her silent. He returned and stood behind her. Without warning, his hands suddenly slid down beneath the top of her dress and over her bare breasts. He pulled them out again. "Stay calm. What can you feel?" He said loudly.

"Your hands are kneading my breasts. How dare you?"

His hands appeared in front of her eyes. "These hands?" He asked. "Or the ones now sliding up your thighs beneath your lovely green dress."

She felt it then, hands reaching up, sliding over her wet skin... "Stop it!" She cried out with a voice so sharp, it travelled across the room like a shard of hard metal, and struck the sphere she had been peering into, shattering it, as fragments spun in the light to the floor.

Veyl clapped his hands slowly. "Well done. An excellent voice command."

Clara no longer felt hands upon her. She twisted in her chair to stare up at him. "Did you put your hands on my bare breasts?"

He said nothing, waited for her mind to work through it.

"Why? Was it to show me some kind of way of warding off witchcraft?"

"My. You're quick to learn. But no. I just wanted to enjoy them; they looked so firm and full of promise. I couldn't resist. It was you who did the rest. We're all full of hidden desires locked in dark dungeons in our minds. You merely agreed, aided by my magical touch, to give yours the keys to the cell door. Your suppressed desires were let loose from Pandora's wet, fleshy, tight box."

His voice had menace in it; his words like fingers tapping her vagina, physical, odd; of course, it wasn't her... was it?

Whatever it was, Clara didn't like it. She stood up, went to the door, opened it, went out and closed it behind her. She sensed, as she put her foot on the metal step, that he was someone who already knew the answers to questions she hadn't thought yet to ask.

Maggie

Chapter 3: Maggie

The door to the study had barely closed behind her when she heard it again—his voice, low, certain, threaded with something that made the fine hairs along her arms stir.

"Miss Merton," he said from behind the door, "you will return immediately."

She turned. And her body was a magnet drawing her towards the dull metal door. It swung open with not the slightest touch of her hand, and the stone interior sucked her in, as though it had breathed and found her the air of life to dwell in its interior and make its heart beat.

Veyl had moved with a predator's quiet from the far end of the room to within a step of her. The lamps behind him threw his face into planes of amber and shadow, his eyes glinting like dark glass.

"I told you," he said, "there are three stages. You have begun the second. Tonight, we move it forward."

Before she could answer, he reached past her and shut the door. The click of the latch was almost inaudible, but the air seemed to notice it, tightening around her like drawn silk.

He gestured to a high-backed chair set before a low table. "Sit."

She did. The emerald dress whispered as it folded beneath her, the fabric clinging at the knees as though reluctant to let her limbs move freely.

Veyl did not sit. He circled behind her, his footsteps slow, measured. "You must understand," he murmured, "that the body is not merely a vessel for thought. It is a network of doors, each with its own key. Chemistry can unlock some. Touch can unlock more."

His fingers settled on her shoulders—not heavy, but possessing that deliberate weight that says I am here, and I will not be moved. He smoothed the fabric there, almost idly, though she felt the warmth of his palms bleed through.

"Close your eyes," he said.

She obeyed.

His hands left her shoulders only to return, fingertips grazing along the line of her collarbones, pausing just at the hollow of her throat. "Every element responds to heat," he said softly, "and every living thing to attention. Even gold softens in the right hands."

Her breath caught—not from the words alone, but from the way his fingertips lingered, touching skin, the ghost of contact.

He moved behind her again. A faint chink of glass; the scent of warm spice and something metallic drifted forward. He placed a small crystal phial before her on the table. Inside, a liquid shimmered like molten copper.

"This," he said, "is for clarity. It will quicken the blood, sharpen the senses. But only when taken in concert with… other stimuli."

She opened her eyes. His hand was still on the phial. The other rested lightly—too lightly—against her breast. It was as if she had whispered 'touch me' there, or he had assumed such.

"Drink." His voice said, but his lips remained shut, a slight smile walking across them.

She lifted the phial. The glass was warm. The liquid burned at first, then bloomed into a strange, heady sweetness. A rush began low in her belly and spiralled upward, into her throat, into her mouth, until even the candlelight seemed to tremble.

Veyl took the empty phial from her and set it aside. Then, without asking, he drew her to her feet.

"Now," he murmured, "we see."

He stood close enough that the fabric of his coat brushed her arms. His hand slid—deliberately, unhurriedly—up under the folds of her dress, resting with the hair of a lioness, fingers parting coarse hair, the way a predator slips through blades of grass on the Savanna towards its victim. He brought his face up to within inches of hers. Their eyes met, and she found it difficult to remember the question she had been about to ask as she gasped, when his hand moved and slid inside her with the ease of a warm blade passing through wax.

"Breathe," he said.

When she did, he leaned forward—not to kiss her, but to speak so near her ear that the words warmed her skin. "Every part of you is already learning to respond. Even if you do not yet know to what."

One hand still inside her, gently moving within an increasing wet interior, his other rose, tracing the line of her jaw, her cheek, brushing just beneath her lower lip with the faintest suggestion of pressure. She felt the echo of it all the way to her fingertips.

"Do you feel it?"

"Yes," she whispered, though the word seemed inadequate.

"Which is warmer, more comforting?"

Against her wishes, her lips parted, "Not the one on my face. The other."

"Good," he said. His hand inside her intimate pocket moved quicker—not roughly, but with the ease of someone certain she would not resist. "Now, keep looking at me."

Her pulse was loud in her ears. The warmth from the phial had become something else entirely, something that made the air between them shimmer and the sensations rippling through her body tell of a promise of heaven that lay in their currents.

Veyl's gaze never wavered. "This is the beginning of the second stage," he said. "When body and mind begin to... co-operate."

And as his fingers spread out, and his wrist twisted and pushed inside her as though he had a contortionist's arm, she felt the strange and thrilling certainty that something inside her had just been... altered.

Veyl's thumb remained at the base of her skull, that point where every nerve seemed to converge. He pressed just enough to make her aware of its power, of the precision with which he could command her to tilt her head this way or that.

"Still," he murmured.

The warmth of him radiated through the silk of the emerald dress, sinking into her skin, as his hand moved rapidly, deeper, now without caring, like a baker working dough, determined to reshape it into his idea.

"You are... receptive," he said. "More than I expected."

Clara's lips parted, though no words came. The air was too thick, too saturated with him—a gasp of intense bliss, not a deep groan, but a gust of warm air through an orchard of orange trees, that caught the sweetness of their scent and carried it away into loftier air, that the Gods themselves might wrap themselves in the bliss from the fruits they'd created. Her legs crumpled with a pleasure too intense for her body to rightly bear, but she never fell. A finger's light touch under her chin held her there, pinned to the air like a butterfly pinned to a display board.

And not once did his eyes blink or move from hers, until his lips fell upon hers, and hers responded in kind under their own intention before her mind could protest. When he pulled back, the pink traitors uttered, "More..." is a voice of a ghost seeking life again.

Then he moved—not abruptly, but with the inevitability of water filling a shape—until his mouth was just at the edge of hers. He did not kiss her again. Instead, he drew a long, slow breath, and she felt it stir the fine hairs along her cheek.

Something inside her seemed to lean forward, hungry for contact to press herself against him, to become one in an embrace of unity.

"Not yet," he whispered, the denial as intimate as a touch. "Anticipation is the crucible. Without it, the metal cools too soon."

Her pulse beat wildly against his fingertips. She thought she could feel it in more than one place—in her vagina, her breasts, neck, her wrists, even deep in her belly.

He removed his hand from inside her; a slow sliding, dead thing, like the skin of a snake leaving its new body, and a slender, vibrant life to nestle deep inside her. She felt her breath catch again, not because of that itself, but because it felt like an answer to a question she had not asked.

"Close your eyes," he said again, and when she obeyed, he leaned closer still, his words ghosting directly into her ear.

His hand fell away completely from her, as a damp finger stroked the side of her face, passed over her lips, coating them with a sliver of sweetness, and enticing her tongue to sweep it away into a welcoming mouth. But the sensation inside her vagina did not fade. It seemed to deepen, as though his deep touch had burned itself permanently into her being, leaving an entrance evermore open and wanting visitors. She opened her eyes. Veyl was already standing half a pace back, watching her with an expression that was not quite satisfaction and not quite hunger—but something between.

"What did you do?" she asked, her voice softer than she meant.

He smiled faintly. "I began your refinement."

And then, almost casually, he turned away, leaving her with the strange and inescapable truth that his nearness was still on her—not just in the place where his hands had been, but everywhere: he was circling her, moving through her, laughing inside her, whispering hunger, screaming more, like an addictr calling for opium to settle their demons.

"You can go now," she heard his voice say through a hall of many corners, an echo that reached her ears after a delay.

When she left the study, her steps were unsteady. Not from weakness, but from the new, unnatural awareness that her body seemed to hum, as though tuned to some frequency only he could hear.

That night, the house seemed to breathe differently.

The long corridors exhaled slow draughts of perfumed air from unseen vents, as though carrying the faint trace of him from room to room.

Clara sat at the small writing desk in her bedroom, the emerald dress draped over the back of the chair like a shed skin. She had tried to distract herself—to write, to read from the leather-bound volume left on the desk—but the sensation Veyl had placed in her had not dimmed.

It was still there, that phantom pressure at her neck and mouth, as if his hands and breath were invisible but constant, moving with her, adjusting their hold when she shifted in her seat. The rhythmic pulsing and twisting within her vagina was there like a faint rippling sensation, faint, but ever-present.

When she touched her own cheek, it was warm. Not the warmth of her own blood, but of an external heat, remembered by the flesh.

She rose and crossed to the mirror.

The reflection watched her in perfect obedience—and yet... she felt observed. Not by herself, but by something behind the glass, leaning closer to see the flicker in her eyes, the subtle quickening of her breath, to feast upon her nakedness.

Her fingertips found her collarbone, traced the line of it slowly. Her breath caught—not from the touch itself, but from the certainty that the movement pleased someone else, so she dropped her hand and stroked her body, opened her legs and rubbed herself gently, now teasing her reflection, and taunting the eyes that she knew were watching her from the other side. She stopped and laughed out loud as she said, "Not now. Return again, another night, and I'll give you a show you'll never forget."

As she spun away to return to the chair and the writing desk, the air thickened. No sound came, but the pressure in the room shifted, like a hand pressing faintly against the door of her mind, and attempting to hold her there in front of the mirror.

Clara backed toward the bed, not sure whether she meant to escape the sensation or surrender to it. When she sat on it, her body leaned forward, unbidden, as if to meet someone who wasn't there.

Her heart was pounding now—and not entirely from fear.

In the corner, the locket caught the lamplight and glimmered. She didn't remember setting it there. And she could have sworn—just before she looked away—that the miniature inside had altered. The lips, once closed, now curved in the smallest, knowing smile. And was that a sound she heard, like a large panel sliding back, and a draft of cold air coming with the shadow from something, nay—someone approaching from behind, as she slipped away from the room, and fell back into blackness as her body fell back to the bed.

It was the sound of morning bird song and the chorus of church bells that stirred her from the dreamless darkness. Her eyes fluttered open, and she looked around to see herself lying on top of the bed. A tap at the door and the voice of Maggie through the oak panels.

"May I enter, please, Miss. Hamilton. I have fresh crumpets and orange juice the master bid me to bring."

"One moment," Clara called out, wondering whether to cross the room to her nightdress flung over a second chair, or whether to fetch the green gown similarly thrown over the chair by the writing dress. But why bother when such boring thoughts could be swept away by events that offered amusement?

"Yes, enter," Clara said, moving herself so she sat on the edge of the bed with her feet flat on the rug, and her legs slightly open. The door swung wide, and Maggie carried in a silver tray, her eyes gazing at Clara's naked form as she crossed the room.

"And how is Miss. Hamilton, this bright Sunday morning?" She asked. "You sleep well, I trust?"

"Like the dead," Clara replied, waiting until Maggie was about to place the tray down on the bedside table, before letting a devil come out of a corner of her insides to amuse itself, as a child might on school holidays, climb a garden fence to scrump an apple, before saying, "Actually, Maggie. I'll have that in bed, please."

"Yes, Madam," Maggie replied, turning. "And that's precisely when Clara did it—lift up to yank the bedcovering back and raise a leg to place her foot on the sheets, and pausing long enough for Maggie's eyes to fall on the centre of her wide open, gaping legs, before lifting the other foot from the floor and letting it down beside the other one on the sheet.

As she flicked the covers back over her, did she see something else flick, like catching the moment when a magician makes a car appear in his hand, snapped there by a mechanism beneath his coat sleeve? Could Maggie really have opened her mouth like a hinge opening fully? Did her tongue flash out, forked and vibrating, extended, and slick itself between her legs, and then was gone. Did a devil inside Maggie just steal the apple that devil inside her had wanted to take for itself?

Clara looked up and stared into Maggie's eyes.

"If you make yourself comfortable, Miss. Hamilton, I'll place this on your lap."

Clara banked the pillows back behind her and rested back, "Thank you, Maggie, and where is Dr Veyl today?"

Maggie bent forward, putting the tray carefully on Clara's lap. She straightened, "There. The master is at first service at St. Thomas's. He goes every Sunday without fail, unless he is poorly."

Clara smelt the warmth of the crumpets drifting up from the plate. She lifted one and bit into it, the butter oozing warm and comforting into her mouth. "Hum, this is delicious," she said.

"Homemade," Maggie said. Confidence and pride in her voice.

Clara bit off some more. "You made them?"

"Yes, a recipe the master gave me. He has a white powder, I added. It makes for bigger bubbles, although no need to add expensive salt after. The powder leaves a taste of salt by itself."

"Draw up a chair, Maggie. Stay and talk with me a while. Would you like the other crumpet?"

"I can sit on the bed if you wish, but no to the crumpet. I had mine earlier, thank you."

She sat and waited for Clara to speak.

"How long have you worked for him?" Clara asked while biting and chewing.

"Since I was a young girl?"

That stunned Clara. Maggie was easily older than the Doctor by a good ten to twenty years.

"But the doctor looks younger. No offence meant."

"And none taken," Maggie replied, her face hiding a brief secret smile as she said, "The Master seems forever to stay the same. He says it's the elixir he takes daily, a concoction of his own making." She paused. "Has he started his teaching of you?"

Was there a touch of jealousy in her voice, a memory in her dark eyes of when, earlier in life, it might have been herself in the study, and the Doctor's hand not beneath a green gown, but a housemaid's black skirt? Clara wondered and thought of pushing it. "Have you ever helped him in his study?"

As her words fell from her lips—like ants teasing a scrap of food between slaps of hard paving—now probing the keeping of forbidden secrets and acts long ago tasted, Maggie face changed; instead of wrinkles and lines writing years across her skin, freckles emerged on cheeks, rosy rich with the blood of youth, beneath jewel eyes which glistened with excitement and expectation. Like a light slowly fading as the oil ran out, it slipped away into a weathered landscape as Maggie answered wistfully, "Yes, when I was a young girl, barely eighteen, when he welcomed me in to help him test something he'd made that day."

Clara started on the second crumpet, ignoring the trickles of butter down over er chin and dripping onto her breasts, like rivulets, looking for the valleys. Were Maggie's eyes swimming in them, Clara wondered as she asked, "A golden liquid? There was so little of it. I remember him holding it up in a slim glass tube and lamplight reflecting back from inside of it, as though it was the sun itself being radiated back to my eyes."

"Did he ask you to drink some of it?"

Maggie's eyes, wherever they were greedily wandering to, snapped back straight and glazed as she held Clara in a vice.

"Yes. A single drop from a pipette."

Clara waited, trying to move her eyes away to look at whatever Maggie's hand was doing that she could hear, but finding it impossible to unlock them from their fixed position, as she heard more clearly, the rustling of cloth, the sound of a small hand turning wet soap, as she said a single word, "And..?"

"It slipped into my young mouth a taste of a summer afternoon, of perfumed flower petals, and the feel of honey as it slid down my too-eager young throat. Oh... How I wanted more," she uttered, as the rustling sped up.

Clara licked her lips, felt herself wetting inside Maggie's telling. The curtains were caught and moved as a gust of wind blew in from a still half-open window...

"I asked him for more, but he told me more is too much. He said, I had to wait for the liquid to seep down to my deepest parts. I recall, even down, his reassuring hand on my cheek as I began to tremble..."

It was driving Clara crazy not being able to see. She could almost feel Maggie's arm moving, it was so active and fervent, could hear the sound of fingers in a jar of treacle, hear Maggie's deepening breath..."

The devil inside Clara, and something new, a thing that had not resided within her until she came here; together, they could hold back no more. As one, it crawled up her throat and snatched her lips, moving them forcefully, "*Let my eyes free. Finish it while I watch you!*"

"Maggie's eyes fell away from holding Clara's. She now peered into just whites; Maggie's eyes had rolled so far back in their sockets that the only thing they could now bear witness to was the memory of her day in the den. Clara's eyes were free, and shot instantly to where the maid called Maggie was no longer a maid, but a self-satisfying wild siren, legs wide open, skirt pushed back, drawers ripped by nails like talons, and a hand beneath the fabric working as dampness spread across the cloth.

"*Go on...*" the devil working Clara's lips said, mesmerizingly in words that demanded obedience, "*...rip those aside and show me. I demand to see.*"

Instantly, Clara watched Maggie's other hand come up with a force which would only have been matched by a Spartan warrior's, as it ripped the cotton drawers, pulling them away as they ripped down the middle to reveal Maggie's hand, swimming in blood and badly torn flesh at the entrance to her vagina. Clara realised she was masturbating herself on flesh. grown old, thin, and pale, was a destructive event, one swapping intense pleasure for that of utter necrotising of one's tissues and organs. Clara should stop it. Instead, she bit more of the crumpet and sipped some of the orange juice, before deciding to put a stop to it. She took a breath, opened her mouth and said, *"Maggie. Use my knife to sharpen the pleasure..."*

It wasn't like anything she was going to say. Who said it? Not me, she thought, *"I said, use the knife..."* her own lips, she was sure now, commanded again. She watched, her chewing ceased, as Maggie's hand shot out and grabbed the knife from the tray. Clara knew its intent. Had the dark thought not sat, briefly, in her mind before levitating itself to her lips?

Clara shot out her hand and grabbed Maggie's wrist as Maggie shook and groaned with a deep pleasure long forgotten and long not felt. The groan gave way to soft words, "Oh, thank you, thank you, my aching body is no longer a burden to occupy."

The hand holding the knife relaxed, and it clattered down onto the metal. Clara let go and watched Maggie's face. Her eyes were now closed, and there was colour in her cheeks once more and the hint of freckles upon skin that tightened over sculptured cheeks. It was as though twenty years were shedding from her face, as she beheld it.

Maggie's eyes opened accusingly as her legs snapped shut like storm shutters before the chaos. She stood up silently, pulled her skirt down and posed more erect as she turned to gaze at the reflection of herself in the mirror. Her hand floated up to her face, her fingers glided over her skin like skiers over smooth snow, and she turned once more and walked to the door, whereupon she turned and threw words across the room like the strands from a cat o' nine tails whip, "You have the voice. Never attempt to use it on him, or the puppet master will swap strings."

She stepped out of the room in such haste that she drew a draft from the room that huffed the heavy oak door to swing closed with the sound of a distant cannon.

A Strange Duo

Chapter 4: A Strange Duo

The slam of the oak door still trembled in the air, a low, wooden thunder that seemed to ripple through the floorboards and up Clara's legs.

She sat very still, the silver tray balanced across her lap, her fingers curled loosely around the half-empty glass of orange juice. The scent of it was sharp now, almost metallic, as though Maggie's breath act of vulgar lust had soured the sweetness.

The room felt different—lighter in one corner, darker in the other—as though the sun had made some secret bargain with a cloud.

On the bedspread, a thread from Maggie's ripped drawers clung to the green fabric like a pale worm, twisting faintly in the draft from the still-open window, a life freed from ancient smells and damp swamps, which now wished, desperately, to fill its lungs with fresh morning air and the joy of life as a free agent, but knowing one of those song birds would soon spot it and steal its life for its own.

The thought stuck like a bone in her throat. Clara peeled it from the fabric and held the thread between her index finger and thumb nails, as you carried it to the window and dropped it out onto the cool breeze.

She watched it float away and soar upwards on a current of warmer air as a house-martin swooped down and snatched it, mistaking it for a hairworm.

She turned her eyes toward the mirror. A tingle in the nape of her neck was buzzing with a warning. And there it was—that something. Not just her reflection. Not just her.

The Clara in the mirror walked towards her straighter, as she approached it; her chin slightly raised, her lips curved in a lazy, knowing half-smile that she herself could feel forming only a heartbeat later, as though her body was following orders from inside the glass.

"You have the voice," Maggie had said

She climbed back into bed, replaced the tray, drank from the glass and set the glass down. The tray wobbled.

The voice.

She tried the shape of it silently in her mouth—not words, just intention—and watched it in the surface of the glass holding the juice, as her reflection's pupils widened, black, drowning our the colour.

The air in the room stirred.

Then—from somewhere below—the faint sound of a door closing. Heavy, deliberate. Followed by the measured pace of a man's footsteps climbing the stairs.

She knew, without knowing how, that it was him.

Her heartbeat slowed to something deeper, heavier.

The steps stopped outside her door.

No knock. No call of her name.

The latch shifted, and the door opened without a sound.

Veyl stood in the gap—not smiling, but with an expression that told her he knew exactly what she had been doing, what she had been thinking, since Maggie had left. His eyes flicked once toward the tray on her lap, then to the reflection in the mirror, as if the two were equally telling.

"Come," he said. Come exactly as you are." And he stepped back into the corridor.

"But I'm not wearing my dress," she protested, but her pleading words fell on ears that were disinterested in her dignity.

"I said, come!"

No room for refusal. The word carried the weight of a hand at her spine, shoving her forward, a fear in her heart to escape an executioner behind her waiting with a noosed rope.

She rose, the emerald dress whispering by the open window as if calling for her to take it, not to leave it behind.

The house was dimmer now. As she walked like a trained, obedient animal at the master's heel, along the hallway and down the stairs, light leaked in through tall windows, but it was the thin, colourless kind that comes before a storm. The air was heavy, charged. Somewhere, a shutter banged once, then again, and dogs—sensing the changing air—barked out warnings to those mortals who had lost much of their animal senses.

Veyl led her not to the study, but deeper—past the long hallway she had never seen fully, to a set of double doors painted a deep, oppressive green.

He pushed them open to reveal a long gallery. Tall windows lined one side, but their light was broken by gauze drapes that turned the afternoon into an amber haze. The other wall was entirely mirrors.

And she was not alone.

At the far end, a man and a woman stood in silence. The woman was young—or made to look young—with hair arranged too perfectly to have been touched by wind. The man, older, had the kind of face that looked carved for scorn.

Veyl gestured her forward. "Our guest," he said to them. "Observe her."

The woman's eyes travelled over Clara with a slowness that made the skin between her shoulder blades prickle. The man's gaze was sharper, like a blade testing the grain of wood. His eyes fell further down her torso, as all men's do, regardless of age. The external look of a female lioness, where a powerful lion might plant the seed of a killing brood, was always too much of a pull for a male to resist.

Why was this happening? Why had he brought her here like offering a morsel, a near-innocent goldfish in a large aquarium that was home to two piranhas—these creatures who now stood before in human disguise.

Veyl moved to stand behind Clara, his voice low in her ear. "Speak to them."

"What am I to say?"

"Anything you wish. But use it. Use what you discovered this morning."

Her mouth was suddenly dry. She looked at the pair in the amber light, their stillness almost statuesque. The words rose in her throat without her consent.

"*Come clo*ser," she said.

The woman obeyed instantly, gliding forward with a faint, dreamlike grace, until her breath stirred the fabric at Clara's shoulder.

The man stayed put.

Clara's lips moved again—she did not think of the words, they simply arrived. "*And you. On your knees.*"

His jaw tightened—and yet he dropped to one knee, then the other, his head bowed as though a great weight had fallen onto it.

A shiver travelled up her spine. Not from fear. From the rightness of it.

Veyl's hand hovered just at the small of her back.

"Good," he murmured. "Now imagine what else you might command, try something they will resist harder."

Outside, the first growl of thunder rolled through the air.

And in the mirrored wall, Clara saw them all—herself standing taller than she felt, the woman beside her flushed and wide-eyed, the kneeling man's fingers digging into his own thighs... and behind them, in the farthest corner of the reflection, a shape that was not in the room at all, leaning forward with interest.

"What should I say?" she asked him in a voice that barely disturbed the dust in the air. The air in the gallery was close now, scented faintly of roses past their prime, sweet turning to rot.

Clara's eyes flicked to the mirrored wall again, but she did not turn her head. That shape—taller than Veyl, broader—lingered in the reflection, still and watchful, as though waiting to be acknowledged.

Veyl's voice brushed her ear.

"Power is not simply in being obeyed," he murmured. "It is in being desired, even when obedience burns."

Clara bent down and whispered something unheard by the others close by. Veyl watched as the woman silently nodded and stood up.

"What did you tell her?" A voice that smelt of schoolroom graphite, smoothed its way up her ear canal and slipped, frictionless, into her brain.

Clara felt that devil and that new thing in her soul break out again and work her mouth, "I told her I knew she could smell me below, and detect the hint of gold in my body. I said I knew how much she desired to lick me there, to taste the elixir of life."

She stifled the devils, but could still not hold them back.

"And..?" the graphite wrote inside her mind.

"I said I would let her drink in full from me, that I would empty my bladder into her throat, fill her stomach, if she did one bidding for me."

The woman had walked back to the man, and was bending down to be level with him.

"And, the master persisted..."

"I ordered her to strangle him until he lay dead at her feet."

The woman beside Clara shifted, her body, lifted her arms.

Clara barked out two words at the man, ***"Don't resist!"***

The woman's hands lifted, trembling slightly, then clutched the man's throat. He did nothing to resist or to stop her, not even when his eyes started bulging, and his face turned blue.

"Enough! Desist!"

Veyl's words boomed through the gallery, out through the walls, corpses in their graves tried to stop rotting, trying to obey his command. The woman let go and rubbed her eyes as though she had woken from sleepwalking. The man coughed repeatedly and gasped, begging the room to pump air into his lungs, as the woman turned, strode up to Clara, stood in front of her, her face, her breath stinging her skin with burning anger.

Her eyes were dark with something that might have been rage, or submission, or desire. Clara felt a strange, delicious pulse in her stomach at the sight. She knew it then in an instant. It was fear, fear of her.

Veyl circled them both slowly, never touching, his presence brushing the air around them like the slow drag of silk across bare skin.

"Do you see?" he asked softly. "They are instruments. You need only choose the tune."

He leaned closer to the woman and, with his lips close to her ear, slipped graphite into her waiting brain.

"What did you say to her?" Clara asked.

"I told her to remove her clothes and fight you to the death."

The woman's hand slipped to her clothes, which seemed to slide off like the skin of an eel being pulled off by the hands of a much-practised, hungry East-Ender.

Clara watched the woman's movements. She seemed to make every small act of her hands and her body like an orchestrated seduction. The woman approached, no sign of fight in her; fingertips grazed the edge of Clara's neck. They barely touched, but Clara felt it—hot copper running down over her breasts, down her body, now dripping like a leaking tap, the dap, dap, dap of her life on the gallery floor and echoing from the distance walls as her senses shot up, and adrenaline shot into her veins at the realisation: the witch had nicked her jugular vein. Clara's breath hitched. It held in her lungs, pushed her young breasts out, and refused to exhale.

She imagined those fingers lower, tracing the line between her breasts—and in the mirror, she saw exactly that, though the woman's hand in the real room had not yet moved. She was merely standing there watching and enjoying the shock in Clara's face as she came to the full knowledge that she had been, in a second, mortally wounded.

Her knees weakened. She steadied herself with a shallow breath. "Kiss me," the woman said to her, and I'll give you your life back.

The lips that met hers were soft, urgent, tasting faintly of wine and something bitter underneath. The kiss deepened before she could decide whether to allow it, and her hands rose to push away, she told herself, but they settled instead on the other woman's waist. The woman's mouth went to Clara's neck, to suckle herself like a greedy piglet around her mother's teat. Clara went to push her away, but found her body wanted something other than that, instead; her hands came up to hold her tighter to her neck, lifting her head back so the greedy piglet could suck harder. In her mind, in a dark cavern of a multi-cell dungeon, where human waste did not just taint the air but filled it with gas that would kill any intruder. Demons, long held in prison, swam inside Clara's body, transforming her biology in an instant. Her bladder emptied into veins filling them with a mix of blood, urea, uric acid, and nitrogenous products. They flow passed through her lungs and heart and were pushed into her arteries; her brain swam and became lost in bright light, and the woman at her neck, on tasting the golden liquid mixed with her blood, sank her teeth deep in Clara's throat, the way a super evolved parasite does, unmoveable, unkillable without infecting that which it was preying upon.

Clara felt the life no longer ebbing from her body: it had become a flood.

Veyl watched from behind. He whispered like a teacher snatching the pupil's pencil away and scribbling the words the stupid child could not recall. She read the words in her mind, as they wrote themselves into the fading bright light, 'Use the voice. Command her to stop'.

"Yes, the voice. She summoned the last of her strength and said in a loud croaking voice, 'Stop. My blood is Mercury. You're already a dead *woman'.*

The woman stopped immediately, pulled her head away, blood across her mouth and lower face, as if a decorator had slapped her hard with a brush load of scarlet paint there.

She clutched her throat, screamed out vulgar words...

Veyl stopped behind between them, "Good," he said, voice like a hand tightening around her spine. "But now—take."

But the command was not to her.

Clara felt her skin turn cold as rough fingers slid down over her bottom and parted her cheeks. A snake the size of a python forced its way in, rough, scaly, unwelcome and intruding where it was not welcome. She felt the thrusting, pulling away and pushing again, trying to work itself ever deeper as ice-cold hands slid around her waist, gripped her stomach and pulled her tighter, like ropes to the tree with the snake anchored to it.

Veyl's hand came up to touch Clara's face on one side, gently pulling her head around to look at him. His words slid out like a helpful friend's. "Clara, you must transform inside, become like carbon, close your biology, knit together those carbon atoms that were structured since birth the way they're formed now. Shift them, or die with evil pushing into your rectum, and your life coating this gallery floor. Here..." A glass phial showed in his hand, which he'd lifted so she could see, "Drink this."

She opened her mouth and he poured it in, a black, soot-tasting liquid. Immediately she'd swallowed it, she felt all her organs shiver inside her body. It was as though they had realised, with great shock of having their illusion shattered, to learn that they were nothing special, just atoms and molecules fixed in stable arrangements—that is, until now. She could see them in her mind, the great tear, the carbon and oxygen pebbling through and rushing out through the ripped fabric. She could see where each carbon molecule had lost its grip on its neighbour, and how she could reunite them.

Veyl watched as he cut in her neck, and the deep bite marks slowly disappeared. I was like her smooth neck had never known suck wounds.

Her body shook to the beat of the man behind her as his snake pretended it was really a steam hammer, attached to a piston. He was enjoying it, this feeling of power and of invading such a beautiful biology. The more it disturbing it was for the victim, the greater his joy, like stealing energy from the other's food, to fill oneself full with their emptiness.

Alas, for his wanting the culmination of his desire to cry out and groan in deep bliss, his snake spitting seed venom into a place which could never be made ready for it, it was not to be, as a circular vice began tightening around the snake's head, preventing forward thrusting and pushing it out. The pain was too much to bear, and he yanked it out.

Veyl's voice came again, low but sharp: "*Stop.*"

Every movement froze. The woman stopped dying and sat still on the floor. The man bowed his head and became like a statue.

Veyl stood before Clara, his eyes fixed on hers. "You feel it now, don't you? The moment between desire and surrender. The storm balanced on the edge of breaking. The transformation we can invoke if we turn our minds inside out."

Outside, thunder cracked, closer this time.

Clara's pulse thudded in her ears. She wanted—she could not say what exactly, but it burned in her like a fever. She was aware of the watching shape in the mirror, every mirror, a presence that followed her wherever she went, leaning closer now, its presence pressing against her skin without touch.

Veyl reached up, took her chin lightly in his fingers, and tilted her face toward him. "The crucible is almost hot enough," he said. "But not yet. Not until you choose to step into the fire."

His thumb brushed her lower lip—and then he stepped back, leaving the air between them colder, emptier.

"*You two, go!*" he said to the man and the woman. They held hands and rushed away down the long gallery and out through the door.

"*Come to the study after nightfall,*" he said to Clara. "And bring the locket."

He turned away, the command hanging in the thick air, and Clara felt the strange truth coil in her chest—that when night came, she would obey. And he would gift her with the power of seduction and a hint of who she really was.

Skin And Bone

Chapter 5: Skin And Bone

It was a stormy night, the sort that turns the whole of London into a single, restless beast.

Wind clawed at the shutters, rain hissed down the panes in silver streaks, and somewhere far above, the sky cracked open with lightning that briefly bled the colour from the world.

Clara stood at her window, watching the black silhouettes of trees sway like dancers in some frenzied ritual. The locket lay in her palm, warm despite the cold draught seeping under the sill. She could feel the faintest thrum through the metal—not the steady beat of a clock, but a pulse, slow and deliberate, as though the thing breathed.

Veyl's words came back to her. "Come to the study after nightfall. Bring the locket."

She had told herself she would decide in her own time, but the longer she stood there, the more the decision seemed to have been made without her consent. But it nagged at her and urged her to go with such strength that she could no longer resist.

The corridor was darker than usual, its gas lamps turned low so that shadows seemed to lean from the walls. She passed no servants; the silence of the house was such that her own breathing seemed loud.

At the end of the lower hall, the spiral of the wrought-iron staircase dropped away into gloom. She descended, the sound of her steps absorbed by the iron as though the house wished to swallow all trace of her.

The heavy door to the study was ajar. Light leaked out, low and golden, and a thread of heat—scented faintly with resin and something sweeter, like ripe figs left too long in the sun—curled around her.

She stepped inside.

The study was transformed. Lamps dimmed to a sultry glow, the air thick and warm. At the far end, Veyl stood beside a long oak table, his back to her, arranging objects she could not yet see.

"You came," he said without turning.

"I did."

"And you brought it?"

She held out the locket and took it over to him. He took it between his fingers, his gaze dropping to it with an expression that was almost reverent—but there was something else in it, too. Possession.

He opened it, glanced at the miniature inside, and for the briefest instant, Clara thought the painted woman's eyes shifted to look at her. Veyl's lips curved faintly. He closed the locket and set it on the table, among the other items: a shallow silver bowl, a decanter of golden liquid, two crystal glasses, and a narrow-bladed knife whose handle gleamed like polished bone.

"Sit," he said.

The chair opposite him was high-backed, its leather warm under her palms as she settled in.

Veyl poured from the decanter, the scent rising in a wave that made her pulse quicken. "Drink," he said, handing her one of the glasses.

She hesitated. "What is it?"

"An opening," he replied simply.

The liquid touched her tongue—honeyed, but with a metallic tang beneath, like copper kissed by fire. It slid down her throat, leaving heat in its wake.

Veyl watched her closely. "Tell me what you feel."

She opened her mouth to speak, but found that her senses were already shifting. The lamplight deepened, edges blurring; the sound of the rain outside seemed both nearer and impossibly far. And she could feel him—not just see him, but sense the precise distance of his body, the weight of his gaze against her skin as surely as a hand.

The knife caught the light. He turned it idly in his fingers. "Some bonds are forged with steel. Other, with sight."

He stepped behind her chair. She felt the warmth of him, close but not touching. The tip of the knife brushed her shoulder lightly—not enough to break the skin, but enough to send a shiver down her spine.

"Close your eyes."

"No." She replied, fearing that hand, the blade, his intention.

"Close your eyes."

He repeated, but now with the voice.

When she did, she felt the air shift—the faint rustle of fabric, the whisper of steps, and then—a second presence. Not Veyl. Closer.

Watching.

"Don't speak," he murmured. "Just see."

A hand, not his, brushed her wrist. Another touched her knee, lingering. Somewhere, very close to her ear, a breath.

When she opened her eyes, the room looked the same, but the chair across from her was no longer empty.

The figure in the chair was a woman.

Her hair, black as a crow's wing, tumbled over bare shoulders. Her dress, if it could be called that, was no more than gauze, clinging damply to her skin as though she had stepped from the rain itself. The lamplight revealed the pale gleam of her collarbones, the shadowed valley between her breasts.

Clara's first thought was that she was impossibly beautiful.

Her second was that she had seen her before. Not in life, but in the locket.

The woman smiled without warmth. It was the sort of smile that closed doors rather than opened them.

Veyl's voice came from behind Clara, low and close enough to thread into her thoughts. "Look at her. Tell me what you see."

Clara swallowed. "Not a she, a he." She replied, her senses deny her sight.

"Close. Not a he or she. It," he corrected softly. "What you see is a vessel. A form shaped to be wanted. Desired. Feared. ·

The woman's gaze moved over Clara with the slow, deliberate hunger of a cat measuring the length of a bird's wing and the vulnerability of its throat. She rose, the gauze of her garment shifting to reveal more than it concealed. Did she see two sexual organs briefly, or were they folds in the cloth?

"You're trembling," Veyl murmured, his hand finally settling on Clara's shoulder, firm and inescapable. "Good. Fear is a fine solvent."

The woman crossed the space between them without sound, stopping so close that Clara could smell her—something floral overlaid with the sharp tang of metal, like roses blooming in a forge, and tinged with musk, like that of a wild beast.

One pale hand lifted, fingers tilting Clara's chin up.

Clara's breath caught.

"You feel her," Veyl said. "How, understand this—she moves because I wish it. She stops when I wish it. The same can be true of you."

The woman's thumb traced Clara's lower lip, slowly, as though committing its shape to memory. Her eyes glinted in the dim light, and for a moment, Clara thought she saw something behind them, not a reflection, but a furtive shadow, watching through her.

Veyl's hand tightened slightly on her shoulder. "Do you want her to touch you?"

Clara didn't answer. She couldn't.

The woman leaned closer, her mouth stopping just shy of Clara's ear. "You already do," she whispered, her voice like warm silk drawn over a blade.

Veyl moved to Clara's other side. She was bracketed between them now, their warmth hemming her in, the air charged to the point of breaking. The rain outside battered the windows, the wind rattled the glass, but inside the study, it was all heat, breath, and proximity.

"Tonight," Veyl said, "You stand at the edge of a threshold. Cross it, and you will not come back unchanged."

The woman's hand slid to Clara's knee, the barest pressure urging her legs apart. Veyl's palm came to rest on the base of her neck, steady, claiming.

Lightning flared through a paved glass lattice, a skylight to the pavement outside, painting their three faces in a single brief, white moment.

"Shall I let her?" Veyl asked.

Clara's knees barely moved, but the gauze woman noticed. She noticed everything. Her lips curved just enough to let Clara know she'd seen the shift and intended to press it.

Veyl's fingers at the base of Clara's neck were still and warm, yet she could feel the latent strength in them, a quiet pressure that said 'You stay exactly where I want you'.

The woman lowered herself to one knee before Clara, the movement unhurried, almost ceremonial. The gauze of her gown brushed the floor like mist curling along stone. She looked up through the dark frame of her lashes, her eyes steady, unblinking.

"She's waiting for your word," Veyl murmured. His voice was so close she felt the vibration of it along her spine. "Say it, and she'll touch you. Stay silent, and she'll simply keep looking. Do you know how long you could endure her looking?"

The woman tilted her head slightly, and her hand—fingers long, nails the faintest suggestion of points—rested on Clara's shin. The contact was feather-light, almost imagined.

Clara's breath deepened without her willing it.

"You see," Veyl said, "most believe temptation is in the act. They are wrong. The true intoxication is in the offering. The question that lives just before the answer."

The woman's hand slid a fraction upward, no more than the width of two fingers. Her gaze never left Clara's. Outside, the storm hurled rain against the glass, the sound like beads flung from a great height.

"Her eyes," Veyl went on, "are not hers. They are mine. Her hands... mine. Her mouth... mine."

The woman's lips parted, and for a moment, Clara thought she might speak. Instead, her breath washed over Clara's knee, warm enough to make the skin there ache with awareness. Her face disappeared, and then her hands. Clara watched unmoving as her green gown seemed to rise at its hem, sliding up to her knees unaided, by her own hands.

Veyl leaned closer, his mouth near enough that his next words seemed to slip directly into her bloodstream. "Imagine what she could do—and remember that it would still be me doing it."

Clara's pulse was wild now, pounding in places she had never noticed before. She felt woman's fingers against her thigh higher, so faintly that Clara almost doubted it had happened—until her skin broke into gooseflesh, and her legs were parting wide all by themselves and there was the faint breath beneath, more like a sound then the moving of air, and a noise like saliva forming in a dogs mouth, overfilling it, and she felt hot sticky liquid fall upon her inner thigh. The thing between her legs, it was over-salivating.

"You have a choice," Veyl said. "You can let her proceed, and she will show you something you cannot forget... as she turns wild and unfettered or you can tell her to stop, and you will live the rest of your life wondering what you denied yourself."

The woman lifted Clara's dress up over her knees, pushing it right up and furling it so everything could be seen by her and Veyl. Its face, its head, an inch from her crotch, not quite touching—an invitation, a threat, both.

Veyl's thumb pressed into the hollow at the base of her skull. "You have three heartbeats to decide."

Outside, thunder rolled across the rooftops, as if marking the count.

The woman's hand crept upward another inch on Clara's inner thigh, and a thumb touched the edge of one side of Clara's Labia, and then a thumb slipped to the edge of the other one, deliberate, as if claiming territory. Clara felt the whisper of gauze against her calf, then the almost unbearable heat radiating from the breath from a mouth that hovered, trembling, a breath away from her wetness, threatening to dry her arid.

She could smell her now—a faint, intoxicating scent like crushed jasmine, burnt sugar, and the after-smell of a spent firework. It coiled around her senses, sweet and faintly scorched, something that felt like both welcome and warning.

Veyl's hand slid from the base of her skull to the side of her throat, his fingers resting lightly against the pulse there. "She knows exactly how fast your heart is beating," he murmured. "And I know exactly how far she can take you before you can't come back."

The woman's gaze lifted to face. Clara saw the brightness of anticipation there, the wet streams falling in long, elastic strings from the corners of her mouth, webs that threaded to the ground, as if to catch lice or spiders and trap them. Clara's gaze caught something then. Her sharpened senses see it the moment it was caught: a tiny mouse had run across the stone floor, straight into the thing between Clara's legs. In panic, it had turned the wrong way. Instead of running out, it had ran in and straight into those gluey threads.

In a moment too short to measure, and too fast for a blinking eye to catch if it closed before the moment, the man/woman/it think sucked, and all the saliva vanished. Clara heard the muted crunch of bones and the lump sliding down the thing's throat.

"Times up," Veyl said. "What's it to be, 'loose or stay'."

Outside, lightning flared, turning the room white for a heartbeat. The woman's eyes caught it, and for that instant, they were molten gold.

"Say the word," Veyl breathed, "and she will begin."

Clara's inner thighs now seemed more alive, the air between touch and not-touch, the decision to begin or stay, so charged she felt more alive than she'd had ever known. Her heart was racing and pounding like it would burst though her chest. Clara's own hands tightened on the arms of the chair, every nerve alight.

"She's waiting," Veyl said. "And so am I."

The woman leaned in, her mouth, her lips brushing Clara's closed vagina as she began salivating again, covering Clara's labia with hot sticky glue that seemed alive and began trespassing, slipping between her vaginal lips and bringing a warm tingling sensation into her interior.

Outside, the storm gathered itself like a predator before the leap. Wind bellowed down the chimneys of the house and the one in the basement study, making the flames in the grate bow and flicker. The scent of rain-wet earth pushed faintly through the cracks in the earth and brickwork, like an uninvited guest.

The woman's lips hovered a breath away from Clara's vagina, close enough that the heat from them seemed to burn through the mound of her lips and melt her insides. Her palms and thumbs trembled—not with hesitation, but with the exquisite restraint of someone who knows that the moment before contact is its own form of power.

Veyl's fingers tightened fractionally at Clara's throat, not choking, but holding her in the exact place he wanted her. "Feel how the air thickens," he murmured. "That is the storm recognising its reflection in you."

Thunder cracked directly overhead, the sound vibrating through the floorboards and into her bones. The woman's breath deepened, and with it came a slow lowering of her head. Clara's skin sang with awareness, each nerve like a wire strung to the point of snapping.

Another flash of lightning poured white light through the tall window, casting all three of them in stark silhouette. For a single, electric second, Clara saw her own body as though it belonged to another: seated, pinned, offered, her face caught between surrender and defiance.

The woman's head fell forward as Clara said, "Loose."

Outside, the storm broke. Rain hammered the glass in a sudden, furious torrent, drowning the street in sound.

Veyl's voice slid into her ear, lower now, darker. "Well done. Now behold."

Clara shivered with over excitement as the woman thing seemed to lose her hair, each shaft retracting back to disappear beneath her scalp. The woman's body seemed to lose muscle and shape until she was unhealthily emaciated, as though no morsel of food had found its way into nourishing her body for months on end. She was all skin and bone. Two skeletal hands with a thin fabric of skin stretched over them moved, parting Clara's labia so forcefully, she feared she would tear.

"Veyl's voice was a comforting whisper in her ear. "You'll never be alone again. A companion will always be not by your side, but even closer, ready at your whim to do your bidding."

It was then that Clara saw the thing of flesh and bone, like a long-legged spider, push her head hard against Clara, wet vulva, until Clara saw it completely disappear. Her lungs snatched air and held it, and her bladder opened, spraying the body of spindles that hung from the neck. Those limbs moved, scampering rapidly and losing grip in the pooling urine, as the rest of the creature disappeared inside her.

"Good. You can close your legs now and put your dress on. I'm taking you out for the evening. A special treat for your bravery and decision. Go and get ready."

"What will I wear?" Clara asked, disbelieving herself that she suddenly showed no concern, that at her own invitation, an indescribable living thing had taken up unfelt residence inside her vagina. Was it possible? Had the liquid Veyl given us, caused her to hallucinate, an illusion, he masterly had orchestrated?

"Not a gown. You must look like a common whore whom I might

have picked up. "We're going to an ale house in the East End."

"Why?" the word fell from her lips like a child's question might fall on a parent's ears, 'why does the sun rise in the sky each dawn?'.

He smiled, but it was not one of warmth, but one of concern. "Because you haven't eaten today. They have excellent pies and a show of sorts. It'll be quite an evening."

He seemed to be warmer, kinder. Was I because she had accepted the dare, the loosing or the staying? "Now go and change and meet me in the hall. Maggie has laid out clothes for you to wear."

The Ten Bells

Chapter 6: The Ten Bells

She met him in the hall. He watched her approach, his head nodding in approval several times. Did the gas lamps flicker and dim each time his head went down?

She could hear the storm outside, still raging. They were going out on a night like this?

"Lift your dress," Veyl said softly, more inquisitive a voice than one of steel.

"Why?" She asked. That word again. The voice of a child. Something moved within her. No longer a child, companion-less. Did she not have it within her to make him answer? *"Why?"* She asked in the voice, despite the maid Maggie, warning her not to.

"You dare the voice on me?" Came the reply like a razor slashing her face. *"Just do it!"*

Not wishing to feel such a painful sting again, she lifted her dress, he looked at her crotch, the white fabric there so tightly gripping her like a claw, that her pubic bulge and the line dividing her labia impressed visibly on the fabric.

"Wet yourself briefly," He said.

A thunderclap outside—white light through the paned thick glass in the window of the door and above it, lit her up like a figure about to self-combust and frightened her so suddenly that her bladder opened and closed. Veyl smiled as he watched a pale yellow patch dampen her, making her vaginal bulge almost completely visible as a colour ink blot upon a white sheet of paper.

She dropped the dress back down. Did he conjure that thunder, light the sky precisely then, to make her carry out his wishes?

"You're ready. Wait here."

He opened the door, and he swept out into torrential rain which seemed to wish to drench him, and feared his power, so bent away as he went to the side of the road. His carriage drew up. His driver in the front seat was clothed in rain gear. Water ran from the brim of his hat, and steam rose from the two strong horses that breathed jets of steam from their nostrils. He turned to her and beckoned as a voice behind her said,

"A dangerous thing to go into the area where the poor are stalked by the rich…"

A light touch on her back pushed her forward. "Best you go. I'll close the door." It was Veyl.

The interior of the carriage was the same little room with the red velvet seats and the faint perfume of oil and leather. She sat on the edge and felt the velvet with her hand as Dr Veyl settled opposite her and hung the lantern so that it cast a pool of light between them.

Something, the taste of metal on her tongue, pulled her hand towards the end of the seat. Her fingers felt here, and sure enough, her tongue tingled with the taste of iron, copper bound together by oxygen. How did she know such things?

She lifted her fingers, looked at their tips, which were red coloured as though she had dipped them in red ink on a stamp pad. The carriage took off, jolting her back into the seat; her hand went out to steady herself and landed heavily where her fingertips had explored. It pressed in wet.

She suddenly felt thirsty. Lightning flashed outside, and thunder rumbled, which joined with the low pitch of his voice. "You'll eat, drink, and dine at a feast shortly. Relax for now."

"What did my hand find?" She asked, still a questioning child.

His lips broke into a knowing smile, "Search for the answer inside. I tire of your asking things now known to you."

She smelled her hand and was oddly drawn to lick it. She did. She licked them clean and loved their odour, and the iron and copper soon to join her own blood. Her mind flashed with pictures each time the interior of the carriage was lit white by the lightning.

The driver… a woman across the seat… he was atop her… an animal encounter of lust.

"You see it, don't you? My driver's weakness. Women at their bleeding moment. He tells me it's to avoid seeding children in the belly of East End whores."

Clara nodded. "You let him do it?"

"Of course. More perks, less pay. I'll fine him though for not cleaning up his mess."

She relaxed, looked out the open window, and saw the rich streets and houses slowly vanishing with the rhythm and speed of the horses hooves. Smooth, well-formed surfaces gave way to cobble and heavy vibration—the horse knew and began their struggle as the rain increased and swirling mist that smelt of sulphur dioxide; rotten eggs suffocated the bent houses and the people she saw crouching in alleyways, or lying in drunken stupor by the side of the road. They were riding through territory familiar to her.

"I sense we're close to the meat market. I can smell the odour of animal blood in the mist." She said. "Smithfield!"

He looked out the window. "We are passing through Blackfriars."

There was a memory stalking her here. She, a child, was being taught to remember her address. Fragments fluttered through her mind like butterflies. Only one carried a name imprinted in black on white, fragile, fluttering wings—Bloomsbury. Born and young here, before… before what?

"We're nearly there. Are you hungry?" Veyl's inquired like a moth joining the butterfly dance in her memory. A feast, a young woman's birthday. She saw them gathered, rich people around a table in a garden… a name… Hampstead… was it a surname or a place?

A thunderous clap and a series of flashes spooked the horses. The carriage stopped as though it had hit a wall, throwing her from her seat to land astride him, Veyl.

His hands snatched her wasp-waist to anchor her safely.

"My driver will steady them. Stay there, if you wish. We'll arrive briefly."

There was a change in his voice. She sensed it, and maybe something else; a longing in the hardness growing like a hill in his lap and pushing against dampness as if seeking a refuge from the storm— but not the one outside in its aerial assault on the docks of London and close by—no, the storm raging within the doctor; an alchemist that still, with all his potions, could not still his own internal torment.

Something moved inside of her, a new thought of her rescuer. She leaned forward, allowing that hill to rise, and she dared to kiss him lightly on the lips. She sensed the screaming and torment, restrained beneath her. She rested back to tease some more. She lifted herself and moved the folds of her dress aside so the hard lump could rest and strain to tear through his trousers and her weak fabric.

"Good," he said. "You've learnt to be in control."

His voice was filled with satisfaction, joy that his primary lessons had worked. Too much, she thought, as she could feel the deafening hunger in every part of him. The Doctor was a vessel waiting to be filled, a fire that needed quenching. How clever and accomplished he hid it.

"I see you," she whispered.

His eyes closed as his lips said, without moving, a whispering… "I want you to."

The carriage pulled up under control. "We're here, Sir," they heard the driver call out.

"Good," Veyl said. "Clara, leave your gown here. You'll go into the Ten Bells as my paid Whore."

The Ten Bells. He took her to the bar and bought drinks. She looked around at this place of warmth. A place with the alley, she often found the shadows to hide her at night, before… before what? It seemed like a distant memory now in a mind of new delight, and maybe, one new, with fears still lingering.

She never saw the phial spilling clear liquid into her glass. Before he passed it to her.

"Gin," he told her. A smile on his face that Santa Claus would be proud to mimic. She sipped it; a warmth moved through her, as she scanned the interior of the bar… men rough and posh… money changing hands or tucked into bloomers or bras barely holding intimate parts from exposure. Was she not dressed equally to those whores over there with men just like Veyl, clothed with their smart suits, hiding rough hearts and aching loins?

He suddenly grabbed her. A whisper slipped from his lips into her gin, and whatever it was mixed with, as she sipped it, the liquid told her, "We need to lure. Men need a sign."

His glass-free hand snatched her crotch. Was she hungry? Yes, starving. She realised it right then. Play along, a bony interior-living mind, told her—a voice from a wet chamber that moved from a dark and moist cell up through the fragile threads in her spine, to spread within an awakening new mind, soaking it.

She spun and kissed him, laughing, showing off, opening her legs and rubbing herself with his hand down there so all could see.

"Good. Well done. Now go to the toilet. The woman now leaving that man behind you is going right now. Follow her. Her man will be just behind her, and the one by the door whose attentions you've attracted."

How did he do it… send words into her mind when he spoke nothing? She felt his hand gripping her crutch tightly. *"You know how much I hunger too?"* She heard from that grip. She kissed his lips one last time and passed her glass into his other waiting hand.

"Yes," her crotch told him—words in the liquid she released through the cotton, that told him… "Later. Our hunger is different."

She left immediately as the woman moved past her.

"Isn't it unique. Nowhere in London have these," the woman told her. "I know the owner. He's a forward thinker. Watch, I'll show you."

She was an East Ender. Clara knew, but a fake one—someone's servant earning on the side. A whisper told her. She watched as the woman plonked her fat arse down on a porcelain chamber that had pipes attached to it. As she sang deep vibrating notes into it, like a Tuba player with a sealed mouth and his trousers down, substituting the air required to make the brass rasp its deep notes, she spoke more: Sorry, too much beer when really I get them to buy me gin. You're new. I've not seen you here before," she said. "Use that one," her head pointed.

Clara looked at the odd, white chamber next to hers. She didn't really need it, but her ears informed her why she was here. Best then to be the spider in the web's centre. She could feel the smooth, deliberate shoes approaching the door and the tap of walking sticks. How many, she deliberated as she pulled her bloomer now and sat on the seat-less rim of this new-fangled chamber pot.

As she pretended to empty her bladder, a voice whispered to her.

Was it the sound of him in the pipes attached to that iron tank above her with the chain dangling? Or was it coming from the bowl beneath her waiting for debris, she could not please it by offering, as she had not eaten...since when?

"Too many come," the whisperer said. *"Control one. The alley outside."*

The door flew open, land laughter burst in. She was ready. Clara knew. Voices had whispered. The woman next to her laughed and farted a trumpet into the porcelain chamber to mask her words as she said, "Take their money first before you open your legs and offer the meat, or they'll cheat you."

Clara's senses rose as the woman's fat thighs opened and closed, briefly displaying red, soft beef, before she stood, her bloomers drawing up, covering it with packaging that only the crown's printed head could prise cotton away to reveal blood-filled steak again—a meal to men's crude appetites.

A fly, a buzz in her ears, as the men closed in towards the lard next to her. The fly won the race. Clara's eyes saw it in slow motion. The slob opened her legs and declared, "Two sovereigns apiece, up front."

But Clara saw the fly had no love of money, only the sweet food now hanging from her and about to fall, unloved by humans, into a white receptacle. The fly flew unerringly between thighs enriched by opulence earned by accepting seed into a syphilis core. Clara could smell the rot growing in the woman she now deserted.

Two of the men went to her, their purses in one hand, their other loosening braces and unbuttoning flies. The third man stayed at the door, smiling at Clara. Her mind spun away, out through the door, out of the Ten Bells, into an alley beside it. She saw what she looked for and returned her mind to her body.

"Not here," she told the man. *"Follow me,"* she said in the voice and wondered if she'd really needed to use it—enamoured as he already was by her beauty and near nakedness. But as the storm still raged outside, she doubted his eagerness to become soaked while he expended his vulgar lust into her body, emptying himself of that which his wealthy wife, all finery and feathered hats, found too coarse to receive. Clara could see her face, her figure, through the man's eyes, not an ugly woman, but one too frail to take the careless pounding he intended to give her.

She led him straight out into the rain, but it was brief as they were in the ale house's side yard below a rusty corrugated tin roof, which provided shelter for the stacks of ale barrels. "You can have me there, she pointed at a store of dry hay, food to replenish the dray horses that pulled the wagons bringing the ale.

"Why not in the modern toilets, I pray ask?" he said, his raised voice to compete with the noise of the thunder.

"More private. Easier to enjoy one's pleasure unrushed." She told him, removing her bloomers and throwing them onto the hay. He stood spellbound, his gaze tied like a taut rope anchored between the grip of her labia.

"My word," he said. "You have such a delectable, pronounced cunt."

"Still tight and little used," she replied with an imp's cat smile.

"Yes. I see you're new here. A cut above the others in your beauty. How much?"

"Two guineas front. Four, rear." The words slipped through red-painted lips, echoed as she opened her legs to secure the price.

"A steep price," he murmured as if about to turn away, but she saw his gaze was still held despite the virtual length of rope now vanished, as if in a dream.

"But you won't be slopping around in a cunt too used. Mine will squeeze the seed from you." Where did these words come from, so coarse both in sound and meaning, words ne'er passing her lips before?

"Done." He said, taking two coins from his leather pocket-purse and offering them to her as he stepped forward.

She was hungry now, the cold pangs of starvation a threat if she did not feast soon. But what she hungered for was not suet and meat, it was copper and iron. She knew he would resist. His manly weight would lend strength to his muscles, would push her away; not yet had she the skill to seduce him to go weak and wait for her kiss, she knew. The thought of failure, became a physical thing which slid down her throat and into her veins, it swam through her body to intimate places, buzzing an alarm and a call for help, opening her vulva wide so a bony 'it' slid out like a large spider and sprang at the man's legs, holding him fixed in a vice of flesh-stretched-over skeleton arms and rooted to the yard.

The shock on his face was the look of the murder victims as they realised their fate. She drifted forward while his mind still battled to understand... how... this thing from her cunt... the grip in its arms... why could he not move...

As her first kiss landed like the kiss of a fruit bat on the artery in his neck. His eyes flew wide open in shock. She heard his scream thoughts, felt his pain, the sharp needle point teeth an inch into his flesh, the vacuum in their calcium honeycomb as she sucked his iron-blood in two streams, direct from his artery into her veins. She drank and sucked with her mouth too, a sound that soon found dominance over the water splashing and cascading off the tin roof, so hungry and greedy was she at her first meal since the transformation.

Silent eyes watched her, a pleased face beneath a brimmed hat— that of the doctor who stood inside the doorway watching her. The thing holding the man lifted its hands and clawed its way up the side of the man, now too weak to move, now too weak to need anchoring. Instead, the 'it' could feed too, the other side, and it plunged its teeth into the other arteries opposite her.

In minutes, they had drunk their fill. *"Inside,"* she barked in the voice and opened her legs wide, remaining still until 'it' had pushed itself back inside.

Lightning flashed, a white and black scene of the yard and the man falling in a heap to the ground. She wiped her mouth and began to put her bloomers back on, watching as the doctor came out and went straight to the man. She saw his shaking head, watched as he turned, came up to her and said, "Never leave them this way, or London will see an epidemic that will swiftly grow and take away your lambs and leave you starving."

His eyes whispered a solution to him. She saw it play out in his dark pupils, a shadow puppet show in negative, a preview of next actions. He drew a knife, the way a magician conjures a wand, turned, bent down to the man, stole his purse, removed the money, discarded the leather, and drew that sharp edge deep across the man's throat. He cut so deeply that the head lolled back to one side, its tendons severed, as the last of his life seeped out and ran off to meander its way between the stacked barrels.

"Come," she heard Veyl's voice in her head. *"We leave that way,"* his arm pointing towards the large wooden gates, chained and padlocked. She followed him as he took hold of the iron lock, and tore it away as the welded chain links burst open as if two banks of horses had pulled them asunder. He pushed the gates open and they left.

She climbed onto the red velvet, soaked through, wondering why he'd remain dry. Did the rain meant for him, instead fall upon her? He saw her shivering.

"Best, remove them," he said, as the horses moved forward, and the carriage lurched. She did, throwing the wet clothes to the floor where they seeped a puddle beneath. The storm outside was ending. Less lightning broke the sky, and the thunder was more a distant roll of drums.

Veyl leant forward, removed his long coat, stepped across to sit on the red velvet beside her. She smelt perfume mixed with graphite and fried bacon, as he wrapped the coat around her shivering body. His powerful arm pulled her into him, his hand came up to slide over her firm breast to hold her lightly beneath her chin. He tilted her head. She looked into those eyes, read their intentions, as his mouth opened and united with hers. She responded in kind, their tongues competing for space to explore each other's interiors.

When she woke, she was in her large four-poster bed, beneath sheets, woollen blankets, and a counterpane... warm... content and at peace with herself. It was a dark, still night, she thought, and wondered about such a strange dream, one so stark and vivid, it could have been a memory itself, had she not seen it was too unnatural to be true. She noticed a sliver of light cast through a gap in the drapes by a gas light, left burning outside in the road by the man paid to extinguish them at midnight; bribed most probably, she thought, by the house-owners, keen to discourage would-be burglars.

Where had they really gone to this very night, she pondered? She recalled no sex show, no banqueting. Had she supped too much gin to recall. She remembers an ale house, people laughing, drinking, rich and poor. There was rain, thunder and lightning, furious and frightening just like in her dream. But she was tired and still weary. She'd ask him tomorrow, she decided, turning over, pulling up the coverings and drifting off to sleep.

The large mirror, that dominated the room, made no noise as it swung open, and a shadow stepped out, putting bare foot onto the floor and then the carpet as it approached the bed. It stood looking down, red eyes in a hooded, long cloak of dark blue velvet. The figure untied the cloak, letting it fall open, so the figure could stand there facing her sleeping head, its body and phallus exposed, if only she woke to see it.

The cloak swung too, the figure turned slowly and noisily, returned to the dark entrance in the wall, stepped in, pulled a handle, and faded away into the corridor there, as the mirror closed to conceal it.

The Price Of Youth

Chapter 7: The Price Of Youth

It was not the knock that woke her, but the faint rattle of porcelain on silver—a tray being carried with the care of someone used to balancing delicate things. Clara's eyes opened to the familiar ceiling of her chamber, washed pale by morning light.

"Good morning, Miss Hamilton," came Maggie's voice from beyond the half-open door. "The master bids you to join him for breakfast in the surgery."

The word caught in her ear. Surgery. It summoned images of blood and scalpels, of broken limbs and fevered faces—but also of Veyl's hands, steady and unhurried, doing things she had not yet decided whether to fear or crave.

She dressed in the dove-grey gown laid across the chair, its cloth still faintly scented with cedar from the wardrobe, and followed the corridor down to the ground floor. The air there was different: not the perfumed warmth of her bedroom, but sharper, touched with the bite of carbolic and something metallic beneath it.

Veyl sat at a long oak table in a side room that seemed part study, part apothecary. Glass-fronted cabinets lined the walls, their shelves crowded with jars of dried herbs, stoppered bottles of liquids in improbable colours, and the gleam of surgical instruments arranged like a jeweller's tools.

He looked up as she entered. "Ah, Clara. Sit." His tone was neither command nor invitation, but something between—as though her compliance was already assumed.

She took the chair opposite him. Maggie was there, just setting the tray down on the table. "Will that be all, Sir?"

He looked up at her, an imp played with his smile. Clara saw Maggie visibly shiver. She had seen such a look before.

"And if I ask you to do something else, would you really do it without question?"

"Of course, Sir. Anything you wish." Clara saw how the words fell out of Maggie's fast, hoping to convince him, so she was not asked to prove it. Clara could hear Maggie's heart start racing; that false smile was trying to hide the weakness appearing in her bladder as fear stirred the liquid there, making it start to boil.

"Anything, you say?"

His words were a blade at her throat.

He turned to Clara and said. "From time to time, I like to prove loyalty so that I'm never betrayed. Best to do it when least expected."

Maggie was now shaking so much that her voice trembled in time as she said, "The Master knows, I'm loyal. Have I not proven it to him, many times?"

"That you have," he told her, his voice friendly, less of a threat. "Please lay out the breakfast."

A cup of coffee, black and steaming, was set before her; beside it, a plate with warm rolls and butter. Maggie did the same for Veyl and then stood there, arms by her side.

"This," he said, gesturing around them, "is where the city comes to be mended… or altered. Rich and poor alike. Some pay in guineas, some in secrets. Some, in other currencies altogether."

She thought of the shadow behind the mirror, the glint of eyes in the dark. "And what am I to do here?"

"One moment…" he said, turning to Maggie. "Could you take that sharp knife, please, Maggie and hold it tightly in your hand?"

She had thought the threat past, Clara thought, but he was just toying with her. Why? His amusement?

Maggie reached out a hand on an arm that someone seemed to have hold of, someone was shaking it so much as to make it impossible to home in on the knife. Veyl watched, his eyes lifting up to smile sat Clara. A small phial appeared in his hand. "Stop, Maggie. Drink this." He passed it to her after removing a small cork.

She took hold of that easily enough, almost as though she knew exactly what it was, and Clara watched as she poured the green liquid into her mouth and swallowed it.

"What is it?" Clara asked.

"Courage and foolhardiness," he replied. My own concoction. Works instantly."

Maggie stopped shivering and shaking. She returned the empty phial. The doctor waited a moment. "Have you noticed, Clara, how much younger she appears now than when you first saw her?"

"Yes, I have," Clara replied, knowing full well what she had witnessed.

"With the patients that come, you'll observe first. Learn what to look for—what's wrong, what can be improved, and what must never be touched. Then, when I judge you ready, you will act. You will find that your... gifts... may serve purposes beyond your own pleasure."

He turned to Maggie, stood up and told her to remain perfectly still. He stroked her face with his fingertips. "I think, Maggie, we should give Clara a demonstration of what potions and suggestion can do."

Clara watched as he picked up the knife and placed it in her hand. "This Maggie can shave years from your skin, if you know the right place to use it."

He pointed. "You know where the small private room is?"

She nodded.

"I showed you once before what to do. Do you recall it?"

"Yes, Master."

"Good, while we eat this delicious breakfast you prepared, go to the private room and return when you finish. I think you should really go to town this time, don't stop until you have swam in the bliss at least twice, and don't make a sound. Not even a whisper, lest you disturb our eating."

Clara suspected what was being asked of her. Had she not witnessed enough damage she'd caused herself down there? A knife. There was profound cruelty in him that he would have her destroy herself so.

As if Veyl had heard her thoughts, his head spun round, like that of a hawk detecting a sparrow moving at the edge of its vision.

"Ah, I see you have witnessed her doing similar already."

It wasn't a question. It was a knowing statement. He started eating, pointing at her plate and saying, ""Eat up, Clara. Patients arrive shortly."

It was as she was finishing the last crumpet, still half of one in her fingers, close to her mouth, that Maggie returned. Clara could hardly believe her eyes. Was this really the same woman? The female who now dropped a knife, covered in scarlet and scraps of flesh, onto the tray, was a beautiful thirty-year-old... no old maid.

"A big improvement. Don't you think, Clara?"

She looked at the floor beneath Maggie, and then behind her, back to the private room. A bloody trail led from there to where she now stood, still dropping small intermittent streamlets of blood to the floor.

Veyl got up, strode to a cupboard, opened a drawer, took something out, an returned. He held in his hands a small pile of wading, which he gave to Maggie. "Here. Go stem the blood, change your underwear, and then return here and mop up. Be quick about it. Patients arrive soon."

The doctor had taken Carla out into the garden. It was an Eden of sorts with the air hanging with perfumes—the smell of Jasmine and lavender, the strongest.

"Why did you tell her to do that?" Clara asked.

"Because she yearned to."

"What, destroy her vagina?"

He laughed. A rare thing to witness, Clara thought.

"No, she hungered for the bliss of orgasm. But every joy has a price. Either you pay for it or someone else." He looked at her, saw his words held little meaning for her. "A smoker enjoys the drug in tobacco. But dismisses the fact that he or she will die of consumption due to it. Lots of small pleasure moments over the years, and then a short period of terrible agony and demise into death."

They talked a while longer. He was treating her more fatherly, kinder, but she knew not why. Did he wish to sleep with her, she wondered? He was older by many years, but when he wasn't menacing, he was fair-looking and quite charming.

"Come," he said after looking at his pocket watch. "The first will arrive at any time."

"The first patients are here," Maggie said. Clara saw she no longer bled on the floor, but she walked oddly. Too much wadding between her legs, probably.

"The gentleman from Hanover Square, and the girl from the riverside," Maggie said.

"Bring the girl first," Veyl replied, rising. He glanced at Clara, a spark of something unreadable in his gaze. "It will interest you to see how the poor present themselves when they believe they've nothing left to lose."

Maggie reappeared, leading in a slip of a girl who could not have been more than eighteen. Her dress was soaked to the knees, the hem heavy with river muck. A faint briny smell clung to her skin, like something pulled from the Thames after too long beneath.

She did not look up, but Clara saw the quick flutter of her pulse at her throat.

"Sit," Veyl said, and the girl obeyed, her hands twisting in her lap.

"She was found on the wharf this morning," Maggie murmured as she withdrew. "Said she'd swallowed half the river and was burning in her chest."

"You may leave us, Maggie," Veyl said.

He crouched before the girl, not touching her, but leaning close enough that his voice was for her ears alone. "I can draw the water from you," he said softly, "but it will mean trusting me... fully."

The girl's breath quickened. Her eyes darted toward the door, then back to him, caught. "If it stops the pain," she whispered.

He stood, moved behind her, and placed his hands lightly on either side of her neck. Clara watched the subtle flex of his fingers, the way the girl's shoulders loosened as though some invisible weight had been lifted.

"You've taken something into you that doesn't belong," Veyl said. "We must coax it out. Slowly. Gently. Otherwise, it will tear you from the inside."

The girl made a small sound—not quite a whimper, not quite a moan—as his thumbs traced down to her collarbones.

"Clara," Veyl said without looking up, "bring me the black vial on the second shelf."

She found it easily, a glass bottle filled with something dark as ink, the liquid's surface catching the lamplight in slow, viscous movements. She handed it to him, and for an instant, his fingers closed over hers— warm, dry, deliberate.

He uncorked the bottle, dipped a glass rod inside, and lifted it dripping to the girl's lips. "Just a drop."

The girl hesitated, then parted her mouth. The liquid slid in, and

Clara could see her throat move as she swallowed.

Almost at once, her pupils widened, her lips parting as if to speak—but no sound came. Veyl's hands tightened fractionally on her shoulders. "Breathe," he instructed. "In… and out."

Veyl moved to the girl's front. He took hold of her dress at the top and pulled hard. It ripped away, leaving the girl sitting there, her pale naked body covered with patches of mud and shivering. The doctor pressed his hand on her lower abdomen, closed his eyes, bunched his finger into a fist and kneaded her like dough. Keeping his fist pressed tightly into her and twisting it one way then the other, he drew it up her body, and between her small, firm breasts.

Clara realised she was leaning forward in her chair, her own breath shallow. Something in the girl's face—the mingling of fear and surrender—sent an echo through her own body.

The girl's head tipped back. A faint flush had risen in her cheeks, and her eyes shone with a kind of fever. He stood up suddenly, opened her mouth with both his hands and locked his open mouth on her; just for a heartbeat, Clara thought she saw a shape, serpent-like bulge in the girl's throat, and then it was gone.

Then the girl shuddered—a full-body tremor—and went utterly still.

Veyl held her a moment longer before breaking his mouth from hers and pushing her back against the chair's backrest. Her breathing was slow now, steady, but her eyes were closed, lashes trembling faintly.

He took two steps away, and she vomited, her mouth gaping wide open, like a piranha about to strike, while a small stream of muddy water arced in the air to splash on the floor. Clara saw it then, a river eel, coiling and writhing across the floor, missing the water to breathe.

Veyl wiped his mouth with a white cloth from his pocket and returned to the girl.

"Rest," he said, as though speaking to someone far away.

He looked at Clara then. "You see? The body yields, the pain subsides, and in the yielding, something new can take root. That is what you will learn."

Outside, a bell tolled the hour. Clara could not tell if it sounded like a beginning… or a warning.

"Can you fetch Maggie to clean up, please. Make a cup of coffee and stay in the kitchen until she returns."

By the time the last of the coffee had cooled in her cup, the riverside girl was gone. Or rather, she had been taken. Maggie had returned without the sound of the front door opening, without the shuffle of departing footsteps, only the faint trace of the girl's river-brine scent lingering in the air. Clara was back in the surgery.

She waited until Veyl was in the adjoining room speaking with the next patient before she slipped into the hallway. The floorboards were bare here, and her steps were near silent as she followed the cold breath of air that seemed to drift from deeper in the house.

It led her to a narrow stair, tucked behind a half-open door she had never noticed before. The wood was darker here, polished by hands that had used it for years, perhaps decades. She descended slowly, the scent changing from the acrid bite of the surgery to something damper, older—stone and still water.

At the bottom, the passage curved into a long, low-ceilinged chamber lit by a single gas lamp. The walls were lined with narrow doors, each with a small iron grate at eye level. She moved to the nearest and peered through.

The room beyond was almost bare. A cot against one wall. A jug and basin. And the girl—the riverside girl—lying on the cot, still naked and dirty, as if in deep sleep. Her chest rose and fell slowly, her lips parted. In the dim light, Clara thought she saw a faint sheen at her throat, like dew on a spider's web.

She turned at the sound of footsteps behind her. Veyl stood in the archway, the gaslight painting a thin edge of gold along his cheekbone.

"Some patients," he said softly, "require observation."

"She's not ill anymore," Clara said, her voice sharper than she intended. "Why is she here?"

"Because she's not finished."

He stepped closer, his hand brushing hers as he passed, the touch both casual and claiming. "The elixir doesn't only mend what is broken. It opens doors. Doors the patient is not yet ready to walk through alone. My work is to guide them... until they can."

"And if they never can?"

His smile was slow, unreadable. "Then they remain here. Sleeping. Dreaming. Waiting for the right hand to wake them."

Something in the way he said the right hand made her stomach tighten. She imagined her own fingers pressing against that warm throat, feeling the pulse under her touch, deciding whether to rouse or still it.

The gaslight flickered. Somewhere above, the bell of St. Thomas's tolled again, muffled by stone and distance.

"Come," Veyl said. "There is more to see today. And soon... one for you."

The next patient was already seated in the surgery when they returned upstairs—a man in his middle years, clothes of good cut but worn at the cuffs, the kind of face that had once commanded a room but now sagged with fatigue.

He rose when Veyl entered, but the doctor motioned him back down. "You've been losing strength," Veyl said, circling him like a tailor measuring for a suit. "Not from any visible wound. No fever. Yet the body tells me it is emptying."

The man gave a humourless laugh. "My wife says I've gone hollow. Says I don't look at her anymore. I can't... feel for her." His eyes flicked away, ashamed. Then they rose and stared at Clara, dropped and fixed on her firm breasts, bra-less, nipples erect and pushing the thin fabric.

Veyl glanced at Clara. "Then perhaps we try a different touch."

He gestured her forward, the space between her and the man narrowing until she could see the pulse beating at the hollow of his throat.

"Stand behind him," Veyl instructed. "Hands here." He guided her fingers to the man's temples. "Feel the warmth?"

She nodded. It was more than warmth—a faint thrum, like placing one's hand on a sleeping animal.

"Now draw it toward you," Veyl murmured. "Not with muscle—with want."

She let her breath slow, her focus sinking into that point beneath her fingertips. The thrum strengthened, as if it recognised her, as if it answered. The man's shoulders sagged, his breath catching in a half-sigh.

"Good," Veyl said, close to her ear now. "You are opening him. Now move to the front, replace your hands. Keep him open. Ignore his words or touch."

The man's head tilted back slightly, his eyes half-lidded. Clara felt a peculiar heat travel up her arms and into her chest—not her own, not entirely his, but something shared. It made her dizzy.

She felt an ache in her breasts; it was as though they were trying to push through the dull gown over them,

She thought of the riverside girl's parted lips, the shimmer at her throat. She thought of the way Veyl's hands had lingered, coaxing surrender without force.

Her fingers slid fractionally lower, brushing the edge of the man's jaw. He shivered.

"Do you feel it?" Veyl asked.

"Yes," she whispered, though she could not have said whether she meant the man's heat… or her own.

The man's hands came up and grasped her breasts.

"You have him, now. Take him," Veyl said, "until you know he's yours."

Her hands tightened, the thrum under her fingers turning into a steady pull, as though a thread had been caught and was unwinding into her. The man made a low sound, something between relief and loss. His hands squeezed her harder, his sharp nails piercing the cloth, pushing into her flesh.

"Take it out of him, through his hands into your breast, your vessels. Use him!" Veyl commanded in the voice. She felt his hands glowing, like they were hot metal fingers, and then burning her, the heat going into her, boiling the blood in small vessels until they burst. But his

arms, she saw, veins bulging and a pulse in them like a pump pushing the blood away from him, into his hands, his swollen fingers, and into her. She bore the pain. It passed. A sense of awe gripped her, made her heart flutter—the knowledge: she had power.

When she finally let go, his eyes were glassy, his colour pale, like someone just waking from a fever dream, but one who had lost blood.

Veyl's hand closed around her wrist. "You see? You can feed without teeth. But it will make you want more."

She did not understand his words, his meaning. She knew she was transformed. No normal woman could live with an emaciated demon housed in their vagina. She was no longer normal, but then what was she?

He released her, and she realised her pulse was racing—not from fear, but from the raw, dangerous pleasure of taking something that wasn't hers and being given it anyway.

The man removed his hands from her breasts.

"You'll slowly feel better," Veyl said. "Go home and rest until morning."

When the man had gone—moving like someone still half-caught in a dream—Veyl returned to his cabinet, replacing vials, straightening jars as though nothing unusual had happened.

"You will learn to measure your appetite," he said without looking at her. "Otherwise, it will measure you."

Maggie appeared in the doorway to announce the next patient, but Veyl waved her away. "That will be all for today. Send them home. Tell them the master will see them when the weather shifts."

Clara knew better than to ask what he meant by when the weather shifts. She simply stood there, feeling the echo of the man's warmth still in her fingertips, the faint residue of his pulse throbbing in her own body. She felt much energy, as though adrenaline had been injected into her.

Veyl's eyes found hers then. "Rest, Clara. And dream. Dreams are the key to deep practice."

She left the surgery and climbed the stairs to her room. The corridor felt longer than it should have, the gas lamps throwing shadows that moved a heartbeat behind her steps.

When she reached her chamber and shut the door, she leaned back against it, her breath catching. Her palms were still tingling. She flexed her fingers slowly, remembering the yielding of her skin beneath the man's, his unconscious surrender of her desire to take his blood, and the man's half-closed eyes, his mind dreaming of her naked and him fondling. She smiled at the thought of him returning home to his wife; his appetite sharpened.

Her reflection in the tall mirror was clearer now, as though the glass had been polished from the inside. The eyes looking back at her seemed almost amused—and hungrier than she wanted to admit.

She crossed to the bed, sitting at its edge. Her hands rested in her lap, but it was impossible not to feel them elsewhere—on a throat, along a jaw, pulling heat from someone into herself.

The hunger stirred again, low in her belly, uncoiling like something that had been patient for too long.

She lay back on the counterpane, staring at the ceiling, and wondered how long she could keep it fed without crossing into teeth and blood. Or had she already crossed that line? Was the dream not a dream at all? How soon would she know?

Outside, the sky was dimming toward another storm, and in the stillness she thought she heard a voice—not Veyl's, not quite her own—a whisper from the glass:

"Soon."

The Lass From The River

Chapter 8: The Lass From The River

It was early evening when Maggie woke her. She had slept for hours.

No gentle knock—just the scrape of the latch, the shuffle of feet, and the smell of oil from the lamp she carried. And something else, yes, disinfectant mixed with dried blood. It came from her, Maggie. Of course, the terrible thing she had done to herself.

"Show me."

Clara said, her curiosity too great to rest.

"What?"

Clara pointed.

"No. It's too dangerous."

"How, so?"

"You... blood."

"*Show me everything*." Clara used the voice.

Maggie's eyes glazed over as she pulled up a chair, lifted her skirt and removed the wadding as she pulled her bloomers off and opened her legs.

"The master could not save the lips, so he amputated them," Maggie told her. "He said they were too badly damaged."

Clara was fascinated. She dropped to her knees between her open legs. Maggie's vagina was an open, bloody steak, still oozing blood. The smell of iron and copper was strong. It drew her head forward as though she was a north pole and she, Maggie, a south pole. Her face was nearly touching, her lips tingling, her throat dry, her stomach empty, and an ache in her muscles the deeper she breathed in the mixture of smells.

Maggie's hand came down onto her forehead to stop final contact. "Don't bite. I don't want transformation."

"*Remove your hand.*"

The hand lifted away. Clara had only meant to briefly lick, a single taste, like the tongue on someone else's sweet. She was surprised herself then, when her mouth opened wide, sealed itself there, and she sucked with all her might, until scabs flicked down her throat, and a torrent of blood filled her mouth and slid down her throat, warm, like honey in its smoothness. She sucked harder as Maggie squealed with pain. Clara couldn't stop. She wanted to sink her teeth in deep.

"Don't bite, I beg you. By all means, drink your fill." Maggie said with pained voice.

'Drink your fill,' she had said. What was my fill?" She sucked harder, faster, until the blood just came without effort, a mighty river of it, filling her stomach full."

She stopped. Looked up at Maggie, as her lifeblood continued splattering onto the floor.

"The wadding, stem the wound," Maggie begged her, pointing to it. Clara passed it to her, wiping her mouth on it first."

She glowed within as she sat on the bed. Your lifeblood is sweet and delicious," she told Maggie.

"Did you bite me?" Maggie asked with a pail face.

"No."

"Thank God. Are you sure?"

Clara nodded, "Yes, I nearly did, my greed was great and I could suck no harder, but then it started gushing out, so no need."

Maggie was no longer listening. She was too busy holding wadding against herself.

"The master wants you in the lower rooms," Maggie said, her voice even, though her eyes slid away. "Now."

Clara dressed quickly, the air sharp against her skin as she pulled on the plain gown. The corridor outside her chamber felt colder than it should, as though the house itself was holding its breath.

Veyl was waiting at the head of the narrow stairs she had discovered, the one leading to the undercroft. His hands were clasped behind his back, his posture precise, like a man about to make a presentation to a patron.

"Today," he said, "you will assist me in... a more delicate matter."

His gaze flicked down the stairwell. "The girl from the river is not yet ready to leave."

Something in his tone made Clara's skin prickle, though she could not have said why. She followed him down, the lamplight brushing the damp stone walls, the air thickening with that mingled scent of still water and something sweeter—like crushed flowers left too long in the heat.

The cell door was already ajar. Inside, the riverside girl sat on the cot, knees drawn up, her head resting against the wall. She looked up as they entered, and for a moment, Clara thought she saw hope flicker there.

"Has the pain gone?" Clara asked, stepping closer, seeing the girl now naked and completely clean with the faint smell of jasmine on her body. Her hair was washed and brushed.

"I had Maggie wash her," Veyl said.

The girl nodded, though her gaze darted to Veyl, then down again, as though afraid of the answer he might give if she spoke.

"Good," Veyl said softly. "Now we must strengthen her. The river took more than water from her—it took her heat, her pulse. We'll return it. But not all at once."

He turned to Clara. "You will sit with her. Take her hands. Speak to her if you like. You will feel her warmth build in you… and you will give some of it back."

Clara frowned. "I thought—"

"You will not harm her," he said, his voice silk over steel. "Quite the opposite. You will give her exactly what she needs. And in so doing, you will learn control."

The girl's hands were small in hers, cold but dry. As Clara's fingers closed around them, she felt the faintest pulse—irregular, but there. She let her own breathing slow, remembering the man in the surgery, the strange, shared heat that had flowed between them.

The girl's lips parted on a breath that trembled.

"Good," Veyl murmured behind her. "She opens easily. Some do."

Clara didn't see him move, but she felt the change in the air—the faint swish of fabric, the shadow falling across them. His hand brushed Clara's shoulder as he stepped around her, crouching before the girl.

"Look at me," he said.

The girl obeyed, her eyes wide now, pupils swallowing the lamplight.

"What happens next," he told her, "is for your healing." His tone was almost kind, but there was something else in it too—something that made Clara's grip on the girl's hands tighten without conscious thought.

Veyl took the girl's chin between his fingers, tilting her head just enough to bare her throat.

"There," he said softly, almost to himself. "Do you see, Clara? How the pulse rises when the body feels both fear and want?"

Clara swallowed, uncertain if what he spoke of belonged to the girl... or to her.

"Keep her open," Veyl instructed. His voice was steady, but there was a faint strain in it now, as though holding back a greater hunger.

The girl's breathing quickened, her hands twitching in Clara's grasp. She tried to pull away, but Clara, almost instinctively, tightened her hold. The warmth she'd felt before was growing now, seeping into her wrists, her chest, down into the hollow of her belly.

Veyl's free hand slid to the girl's shoulder, pressing her back against the damp wall. The movement seemed casual, but the pressure was unmistakable—controlling, claiming.

"You feel it, don't you?" he murmured to the girl. "The way your body answers, even when your mind protests. It's the truth beneath the skin."

He glanced at Clara. "More, if you please."

Clara drew in a slow breath and let her focus narrow to that thrum beneath her palms. It responded instantly, the girl's pulse jumping, her breath hitching.

Veyl's other hand moved down now, resting over the girl's heart. His thumb traced a small circle, again and again, until the girl's eyes half-closed. Then his fingers spread, splaying across her chest, pressing—not hard enough to bruise, but with a weight that pinned her in place.

He produced a phial. It was larger than the usual ones he made appear at such moments. He popped the cork off. You can let her go now," Veyl said.

She did. "Here, he said to the girl, drink this."

"What is it?" The girl asked, taking it.

"An elixir," he told her, a smile hiding his lies, "It will make you feel better, less cold, less sore inside."

She drank some of it and smiled. "It's nice, like candy."

"Finish it," he said. She did and returned the phial.

Clara could not see what Veyl did next. His body blocked the girl and his hands from view.

The girl made a small, desperate sound, and Veyl's gaze sharpened.

"That's it," he said. "The body tells the truth."

He leaned in then, his mouth close to the girl's ear. Clara couldn't hear what he whispered, but the girl's reaction was immediate—a sharp gasp, her body stiffening, then sagging as though something inside her had uncoiled.

Veyl's hand slid lower. The movement was deliberate, the kind of touch that would have been intimate in a lover, but here... it was something else. Clinical, yes—but threaded through with cruelty, the way a predator might toy with prey before the bite.

Clara's eyes faltered, and for a heartbeat, the girl's eyes locked with hers—pleading, though her lips remained parted in a breathless tremor.

Veyl didn't look up. "Go now, Clara. This is not for your eyes. Leave and don't come back."

Clara got up and left. He came over, closed, and locked the grille.

He smiled through the lattice iron as he removed his clothes and stood there naked, his penis erect and as huge as a giant's. My lust for you grew too great. The girl is to save you from me. Now go. Be quick, or I'll drag you in here and do you both."

He pointed. She knew it was for her best and walked the passage back to the stairs. She waited at the foot of them, heard the girl's soft voice say, "What are you doing? Why can't I move? Please, that's hurting. I'm too small."

And then that awful scream, like an animal finding its leg caught in a bear trap.

The gas lamp hissed, its light catching on the wet gleam of Clara's eyes as she imagined the horror the young woman was experiencing.

"Don't," he said, quiet but sharp. "It will only be worse if you fight me." She heard Veyl say. Then quiet, except for the heavy pounding and bedsprings being stretched to the limit.

Clara climbed the stairs and slipped out into the garden, her skirts whispering against the damp grass. The night air bit at her skin, cool and clean compared to the cloying heat of the surgery and the horror she had just witnessed downstairs. She needed distance, even if it was only a few steps beyond the walls. The scent of wet earth and the faint tang of the Thames drifted on the breeze, soothing the churn in her stomach.

She wandered toward the edge of the lawn, letting the shadow of the great yew tree fall over her. Somewhere high above, a nightjar trilled once, then fell silent. The whole garden seemed to hold its breath.

Movement tugged at the edge of her vision—just a flicker at first, no more than a ripple in the darkness clinging to the side of the house. She turned her head slightly, cautious, unwilling to be obvious. There, half-shrouded in shadow, was a thin figure pressed against the brickwork three floors above.

At first, she thought it wore a cloak, the black folds hanging still against the pale stone. But the cloak shifted—too fluid, too alive—spreading slightly, catching a thin glimmer of moonlight.

A gap in the clouds passed overhead, and the silver light washed across the figure. Her breath stopped in her throat. Not a cloak—wings.

They were vast and membranous, webbed like a bat's, their edges tattered yet strong. The figure's head tilted, revealing a pale face framed by the curve of those wings, eyes reflecting the moon in a way no human's could. It was climbing—not with hands and feet but with talons that bit into the wall itself—moving silently toward the very window of her bedroom.

She pressed herself back into the shadow of the yew, heart hammering, yet unable to look away.

Halfway up the wall, the creature paused, turning its gaze down to her. She felt the weight of it like a hand on the back of her neck—assessing her, not as prey, but as something… something… something else. The corners of its mouth lifted, a subtle, knowing expression. Then, impossibly, it pushed away from the wall.

The wings spread to their full span, blotting out the moon for a heartbeat. It glided soundlessly over the garden, descending in a slow arc until it landed no more than ten paces from where she stood.

It straightened, folding its wings close until they looked almost like the folds of a greatcoat again.

"Clara Merton," it said—her name shaped by a voice like dry leaves rustling. "I have been waiting."

She wanted to step back, but her feet betrayed her, holding her ground. "You know me?"

"I know what he has made you," the figure said. "And I know what he will take from you, if you let him."

The air between them seemed to grow colder, but the fear inside her was shifting—turning, hardening into something closer to curiosity.

"What are you?" she asked.

Its head tilted again, and in the moonlight, she saw that its pupils were vertical slits, like a cat's. "A survivor," it said. "And if you choose—your ally."

Clara's fingers tightened on the folds of her gown, though she kept her chin high.

"What would you want with me?" she asked.

"Want?" The figure gave a faint, humourless laugh. "You mistake me for him. I do not own what I hunt. Nor what I protect."

"You protect people?"

"Only those who stand at the edge," he said, taking a slow step forward. The grass did not stir under his bare, clawed feet. "You stand there now—half in his world, half in your own. But you cannot remain balanced forever."

She thought of Veyl's hands on the girl's throat, the heat in her own palms, the dizzying rush that had followed. "And you would... pull me back?"

His eyes narrowed slightly. "No. I would push you through... and teach you how not to drown in it."

The wings flexed faintly, catching the moonlight in a way that made the skin between their bones shimmer. "You think him your master, but he is only a keeper. He keeps the young in cages until they ripen. He will feed on you in time—not your blood alone, but your will. And once that is gone, you will obey even when you hate him."

Her mouth was dry. "How do you know this?"

"Because," the figure said, and in a blink, he was closer, his shadow falling over her, "I was in his cage once."

A strange scent reached her—iron and storm water—and she realised he smelled faintly of the night air over rooftops. "What do you want from me?"

"Only this," he said. "When you feel the cage begin to close, call for me. I will come. But understand—my protection is not without its price."

"And that is?"

He leaned closer, so that the edges of his wings framed her face in darkness. "One night," he said softly, "you will drink from me. And when you do… you will never be his again."

Something in her stomach twisted—fear, yes, but threaded with the same dangerous pull she'd felt in the surgery. She wondered what his blood might taste like, what it might do to her.

The figure stepped back, and the cold night air rushed in between them. "When the moon wanes, I will return," he said. "Be ready."

Without another word, he unfurled his wings in a single, sweeping motion. The rush of air stirred the leaves overhead, and then he rose, impossibly fast, vanishing into the black seam between roof and sky.

Clara stood there long after he was gone, her heart pounding. In the dark glass of her bedroom window above, she could see her own reflection looking down at her, like a mind echo, or a ghost—and, just for a moment, she thought she saw those black wings framing her shoulders. She felt something else, fluid falling from her vagina.

By the time Clara stepped back into the house, the air inside seemed thicker, pressing against her skin like damp velvet. The corridors were hushed. Only the longcase clock in the hall broke the silence, each tick heavy and deliberate, like the measured beat of something alive.

She climbed the stairs slowly, pausing on each landing to listen. No murmur of Veyl's voice, no rustle of Maggie's skirts—only that heavy stillness, as though the whole house had slipped into a breathless pause. And yet Clara doubted it ever truly slept.

Her room was exactly as she had left it—the curtains drawn tight, the counterpane perfectly smoothed. She closed the door, turned the bolt, and stood still, breathing in the faint scent of rosewater from the linens. But there was something beneath it… something cooler.

Night air. Damp. Metallic.

She moved to the window and eased the curtain aside. The garden lay in deep shadow, the yew's branches curling black against the pale sweep of the moonlit lawn.

A movement caught the edge of her vision. She turned her head sharply—nothing. The grass lay undisturbed. The bricks of the wall were bare.

Still, the fine hairs on her nape prickled.

Her gaze climbed the face of the building toward the roofline. For a long moment, only the pale geometry of stone and shadow met her eyes—until a shape shifted. Small at first, but wrong for any bird or man. Wings half-folded, clinging to the gutter like some gargoyle broken free from its pedestal.

Then the moonlight caught its face—or rather, its eyes. Two pale, unblinking disks, fixed on her.

She did not look away.

She did not flinch.

It tilted its head, a slow, deliberate motion, like a predator weighing the moment before the strike. Then, without sound, it slipped over the edge and vanished.

A faint thud came from the terrace below. The soft scrape of talons on stone. Then silence.

She turned from the window, her pulse in her throat, crossed to the bed, and slid beneath the covers. The mirror opposite reflected only her own pale face.

Minutes passed. Nothing moved.

Just as sleep began to pull at her, the faintest impression—less a sound than a sensation—brushed her mind. Not words, but a presence. I am here.

Her lips curved before she realised she was smiling.

It was sometime past midnight when she woke again, though she couldn't say why. The darkness felt heavier. Then she heard it—soft, deliberate—a faint scuff, the kind of sound a small bird might make when trapped indoors, or a mouse nosing the boundary between carpet and bare wood.

She lay still, feigning sleep, peering through her lashes.

The mirror was swinging open. Behind it, the narrow blackness of a secret passage yawned, the air within cooler still. Something had been watching her from the other side of the glass.

A figure emerged, cloaked in deep blue, hood drawn so far forward that only the glimmer of two eyes showed—eyes like embers in shadow. It moved to her bedside. The cloak parted.

It was a man. Naked beneath. A large erect penis, inches from her face.

Her first thought—absurd, almost wicked—was of a stage farce: the phantom flasher, haunting sleeping women.

Impulse overtook her. She sat bolt upright. "Boo! Caught you."

He recoiled like a child scolded, clutching his chest. "Ooo... oo... oo—my heart, it's going to stop..."

Clara giggled. He was no threat.

"Sit down," she said, patting the bed. "Recover yourself."

He obeyed, still panting.

"And put that thing away," she said pointing, at the still stiff phallus.

"What?" he said, grabbing hold of it. "There's nowhere to put it."

"She giggled. "Well just make it go flaccid."

"I can't. It's permanently that way."

She giggled again.

"Please don't make fun of me. It's not my fault."

"I see. May I hold it?"

"Why?"

"It looks unreal."

"If you must."

She gripped it in her hand, her fingers and thumb wrapping tightly around it. She tried to pull it down...

"Ooo... ooo... oo.." He screeched out.

She let go, and it slapped back hard against his stomach.

"How did it happen?"

"Veyl."

Her mirth softened into curiosity. "Always?"

"Yes."

Her smile faltered. "Why are you behind the mirror?"

"Hiding. He thinks me dead. He doesn't know the passage connects to the sealed attic next door."

Before she could ask more, he lifted a hand. "Ssshh—footsteps."

In a swift motion, the cloak swung closed around him and he vanished into the passage. The mirror settled silently back into place just as the door opened.

Maggie stepped in, candle in hand. "May I speak with you?"

"Of course," Clara said, still half-reeling from the encounter. "Where's the master?"

"Out. We won't see him until midday tomorrow."

"Where is

Maggie's eyes dropped. "East End. To feed."

"What ale house stays open all night?" Clara asked with mock innocence.

Maggie gave a sharp, humourless laugh. "He feeds on people, silly."

Clara let the silence stretch after Maggie's words, the faint hiss of the candle wick the only sound.

"Feeds," she repeated softly, tasting the word. "On people."

Maggie's mouth tightened. "You'll see soon enough. Best not to ask before you must."

The Maid's Request

Chapter 9: The Maid's Request

"How's your wound?" Clara asked.

"Bad. It was stable until you drank from me. Thank you not for biting."

Clara tasted iron and copper as the beautiful memory of it returned. "I'm not sorry," she said. "I hadn't meant to, but you smelt, you tasted... like nothing I tasted before—divine."

Maggie leant back lightly. Clara heard her heart skip a bit. But she mustered courage, "I did not come here now to let you grow stronger and take nutrients that way from me, again."

Clara could smell the blood. No uniform cloth, wadding, or fragile bloomers could trap the scent. "Why are you here then?"

"I came to trade. It's a high-risk thing to me, but a desperate gamble."

"I have nothing to trade with. I have no money." Clara said.

Maggie looked up at her, a fire in her eyes that Clara had never seen before. "I want something from you, and I can give you something in return."

"What can you give me?"

"He's only half transformed you. I can give you my secret so he will never bite you. That would take you over, and you'll forever belong to him. It's why I am not fully transformed. Yes, he commands me, forces me to have sex with him, careless and violent. He feeds from me, but not with a bite as I repel him that way."

An owl called outside in the dark, a lost mate... a hope to find a new one. It distracted Clara. Her hearing now so acute, she heard its wing brush the leaves on the branch it rested on, as it took to flight.

She looked at the candles and the oil lights and wondered if those flames were really the life finally escaping the oil it was made from.

She turned back to Maggie. "What is it you want?"

"I was sixteen when he entrapped me. A mere four years ago."

It was an ad in a local paper, the one I used with others to make a bed on the streets. I was orphaned to them when my parent died poor."

Clara listened patiently, trying not to focus on the aroma of blood from her.

I grew old with him feeding on me. He would cut a vein or an artery, oh so slightly, push a narrow tube in, scare me so my heart pumped harder, and then sucked at his end of the tube. If he took too much, which he often did, I would pass out. I lay for days until I recovered, and he would rape my body while I was that way. It aged me."

Something in the night snatched the owl mid-flight. Clara heard it—a creature of stronger, bigger wings, something that sucked the life from it.

"You can restore me to my age, now twenty-two," Maggie continued.

"How?" Clara asked.

"Orgasm strips my years. He made it that way, hoping it would entice me to have asex with him more readily. I never have. He's nothing but evil"

"Can you not cause it yourself?"

"Only by extremes, as you've witnessed. It's a thing of the mind. One needs to teeter on the edge of danger or the promise of conception. You could do that to me. With you, I could teeter on the edge of utter destruction if you bite, or a complete return to my real self, so I can run away if you don't"

Clara's interest picked up. A fine meal was offering itself in the hope of resurrection. "What, you want me to give you an orgasm?"

The air stirred in the room. It was then she heard the sucking outside, distant, and then the flapping of a large bat... nay... it was him, the young man with large wings.

"Yes," Maggie said.

Clara loved that moment earlier, her mouth sealed, tasting and consuming blood mixed with the sexual juices of a woman. It was exquisite.

"I am having my period. You can drink from it, the richest blood, full of iron, but you must not bite or take too much or you'll kill me and never get the secret that will prevent you from becoming his."

"Won't your wound open more?"

"No," Maggie said. "Not if you take that blood, which is natural and do it in a delicate way, while you use your tongue to bring me to the bliss."

Clara was tempted, but it was not enough.

"When I've orgasmed, I will give you the secret that'll stop you becoming his slave."

The words of the young man in the garden rang again in Clara's head. "One night," he said softly, "you will drink from me. And when you do… you will never be his again."

"The master intends to drink from you the day after tomorrow. He told me."

Clara looked at her. Her mind spun. She was caught in a trap, one woven by Veyl. Was this a way out?

"Blow out the light," she said, folding back the sheet, the blanket and the counterpane. "Remove your clothes, your wadding, and get in beside me."

She felt Maggie's heart quicken, heard the breath of the man behind the mirror watching them.

"Actually, leave the light on, that we may see," Clara said, knowing full well that the blue-cloak man would see all.

"I'll change the sheets out and wash them, come morning," Maggie said. "He'll not know."

"Please, Maggie, undress in front of the mirror," Clara said.

"Why?"

"So I can see the front of you and the rear of you at the same time. I'm trying to fix myself on sexual appetite, rather than blood lust, so I don't err." She lied, knowing she was giving a gift to the blue-cloak man. As Maggie undressed, Clara asked, "What happens if I bite you?"

Maggie turned from the mirror to face her. "You won't stop until I'm drained and dead. You'll try to feed on him, and then you'll be his— stuck here forever for him to brutalise you sexually, two, maybe three times a week, as you will be what he's always longed for, his mistress."

"Come into bed. I won't bite you," Clara said.

Maggie approached the bed.

That sweet, beautiful smell again, Clara thought, growing stronger with every step Maggie took. It wasn't just the copper and the iron; it was the hormones, the sour smell of her vaginal interior, mixing with the smell of blood; they went together, the odour of life, organic matter, promise of renewal through conception and birth; and the metal helping oxygen become attached to red blood cells. Clara glowed inside, her heart beat faster as Maggie climbed into bed, and Clara pulled her body into her, a shiver of excitement running through her as their bodies became one.

As if to encourage her, Maggie started kissing Clara, her soft lips and open mouth, welcoming and wet. "This is lovely, Maggie. You're warm, soft, and make me feel comforted."

Maggie stroked the back of Clara's head, letting her fingers play in her hair. "Let me see if I can make this better for you," Maggie said, and slipped away under the covers. Clara felt it then, a wet tongue against her clitoris, gently arousing her, giving her small waves of pleasure and fanning the flames of sexual hunger. She did it for a while and then slipped back up again to kiss her. She tasted of sex, of lust, pushing her tongue deep into Clara's mouth.

Clara broke the kiss and slid under the coverings, her tongue leaving a wet trail down Maggie's body, over her firm breasts, her naval...

Maggie's hands fell upon the back of Clara's head, pushing her down as Maggie opened her legs until Clara's face nestled there, her mouth against the hot red blood seeping from her.

Clara's heart raced and pounded in her chest as she swallowed, lashed out with her tongue, pulled away from the temptation to plunge her teeth into blood-gorged, tender meat, and instead flicked it rapidly against Maggie's clitoris and circled it. She felt Maggie writhing and her hands pushing her head harder against her, until Maggie was like a lover making love with Clara's face.

But a temptation came in waves, the desire to be at the food source, the iron, the copper—the blood. Yet, each time Clara went to slip those few inches lower, Maggie would gently but firmly pin her head to where it was, preventing her from reaching or biting.

It was a battle, a conflict in Clara's mind. She wanted to taste the blood, to feel the hot juice in her throat, and Maggie seemed to know exactly when to relax the pressure on her head, so she could indeed slide down and drink from her briefly, before Maggie's hands coaxed her away again, and back to continue stimulating her, and before she bit.

It went on for a while with Maggie writhing faster, harder, until she groaned loudly, and Clara felt Maggie's entire body go into blissful spasms, as she orgasmed, and then went quiet and still. The pressure on Clara's head disappeared, and she was free, free to slip down, to close her mouth against Maggie's permanently open, labia-less vagina, and to seal it as she gently sucked what was inside... oh, that blissful cocktail of vaginal fluid, blood, and placenta debris... and like honey, feel it slip down her throat. But it wasn't enough. She wanted more. She felt her dog teeth growing, making it so she had to open her mouth wide to prevent them from pushing through her own tissues. She raised her head, her neck stretching back, poised now, a foot away from the meal of a lifetime, a food that not just beckoned but screamed at her: *eat me, eat me... eat!*

She could smell the night outside, hear the fluttering of distant moths, smell the sap in the leaves of the trees, the odour of fish and eels in the Thames. She craved to let her raised head fall, to close her mouth like a deadly, inescapable, jagged, steel trap, to hold Maggie in her mouth, and draw from her as though she was an overloaded sponge.

"Please don't," she heard Maggie whisper, as Clara felt the coverings being pulled completely away, sensed Maggie's eyes watching her; but her hands never came to pull her away—she was waiting... waiting to see if my head will fall and commit, or if I will conquer my craving and move away from this fateful moment, Clara thought.

She breathed in the smell, that odour, rising on the warm air from Maggie's hot, open crotch; taking the aroma from nostril into lung, from lung into blood, into her veins and arteries, and then into her soul. She was weakening... *bite... take the bitches blood... empty her...* a demon inside her screamed. A hand touched her then—Maggie's hand, gentle, stroking her head..."

"Oh, our beautiful Clara. What has he done to you? Bite, if you must; if the craving is breaking you. Empty me if you do; leave not a drop in my veins, or I will forever be doing the same to others."

Her hand stroked Clara, Maggie's soothing hand; her heart felt her torment, empathised, loved her. Clara knew. She knew Maggie cared…

Clara's teeth retracted, and she closed her mouth, drawing herself up to be face to face with Maggie, whereupon she stroked her smooth cheek and gently kissed her. "Please don't run away too soon. I need a friend."

Maggie spoke softly. "I must flee before he sees me young again, or he'll know it was you, and his wrath is more than his bite. He'll flog you, strip your flesh from your body. You yet don't know the extent of his evil."

"I know where you can hide," Clara said. "A place he'll never find you."

Maggie reached over and turned up the oil lamp. Clara saw now, not a thirty-plus woman lying beneath her, but one barely out of her teenage years, young, beautiful, perfect. She was looking at her with eyes filled with curiosity and hope.

"Where?"

The faintest of clicks. They both twisted over on the bed as a gust of air flung fresh odours into the room, and Clara heard a third beating heart. A pair of glowing eyes, peering out of a gas-lit narrow passage, an opening beside the swung-back mirror.

"I know that voice." Maggie blurted out. "Eric, sweet boy. Can it really be you?"

"Yes. Still with the face of a beast and a permanent aching erection since I drank the devil's potion."

Maggie got out of bed, dropping blood as she crossed the room.

"Maggie. Wadding. You're leaving a trail."

She turned and saw.

"Here, catch," Clara called out and flung a heap of wadding to her. "I'll get the water jug and wash that up."

She listened as she worked, mopping the floor with a cotton vest soaked in water. When finished, she weed on the floor where the blood had been to mask any faint odour of metal, should Veyl sense it. She took another clean cotton vest and worked the carpet, listening all the time to Maggie and Eric.

He explained to her how he'd found the mirror to be a secret door. The house's previous owner had used it to keep precious goods in—

money, paintings, and cheeses. He had once owned both houses. The attic had no trapdoor to the house beneath it and was adjacent to Veyl's large house.

Eric explained how he would come out of the attic, through the bedroom, out the window, and down a metal fire escape at the side of the house to go to the markets, face hidden, and buy food.

"Where did you get the money from?" Clara heard Maggie ask.

"The owner must have died with his secret intact." Maggie heard. "The attic is filled with chests of sovereigns and jewellery."

Eric took Maggie's hand and walked up to Clara as she stood up.

"Show me your face, Eric." She said.

"No. It will scare you badly. Veyl saw it as a little prank. The potion he made has a permanent effect which can only be reversed by an act no one would have strong enough a heart to do."

"Show me." Clara used the voice on him.

Immediately, she gasped aloud and her heart skipped several beats. She felt sick and faint as she beheld a face with missing lips and half a nose gone. Saliva and snot ran in continuous streams down onto his body, where they coated it with a shiny wet varnish, in which specs of green and yellow swam, merged, and parted like leaf fragments on the surface of a stagnant pond, moved only by the breeze above it.

"Eric can only be restored by a beautiful woman sharing an orgasm with him. I tried for him and indeed, he felt the bliss, but look at him—I just could not reach that point. I'd spent the entire act fighting myself so as not to vomit." Maggie told her.

Clara sat back on the side of the bed as Eric went to replace the hood. "Leave it," she told him. "Let me become used to seeing you, as Maggie seems to have done."

"You could help him. He has a pure heart. Timid and kind."

"I help him? How?"

"Have sex with him."

Clara was nearly instantly sick. She heaved loudly several times before she won the battle over her stomach's desire.

"It needs to be done tonight, before the devil returns. You're stronger than me. You could end his suffering."

"Don't, Maggie. Can't you see? You're making her sick. It's all she can do to hold it back."

Clara decided to steer it away from such horror. "Maggie. You owe me still regarding our trade."

"What? God, yes. Sorry, I'd forgotten. You must eat garlic, at least three cloves raw each day, so it stays in your blood. He may still bite, but at the first taste, it'll burn his mouth and stomach like sulphuric acid. He will not take more or enough to change you forever."

Maggie went to her clothes still on the floor, holding the wadding tightly against herself all the time. She fished in the pocket and brought something out.

"Here. Take these. There's more in the kitchen pantry, and a man at the local market always makes sure he has a good supply for me every Saturday morning. The first time you take it is like being poisoned. Likely, you'll be sick and fall asleep. But after, it won't happen again."

Clara looked to see as she took them—three bulbs of garlic.

"Thank you. I need to sleep and rest now. I'll explain the blood in my bed as my period, and me being caught by it unaware. Go with Eric."

She lifted her legs onto the bed and pulled the covers up over her, as she watched Maggie walk hand-in-hand with Eric to the mirror. Maggie stepped into the passage first, as Clara turned out the oil lamp, causing sudden heavy darkness.

"Eric," she called out in a soft voice. "Close the mirror and come to my bed. Let's see if I can make you whole again."

Eric, The Lover

Chapter 10: Eric, The Lover

She heard his footsteps in the pitch black, and then a stirring inside her—not one of a fluttering heart, or a vaginal reaction to what was coming. Of course, she thought, 'it' was still in there... in her vagina.

The darkness pressed close, heavy as wet velvet. Clara's ears caught the faint shuffle—Eric's approach through the black. Her body trembled, but not from the innocent shiver of a maiden waiting on her lover. No, the tremor came from deeper, from the presence she still carried inside her womb: it—that parasite of bone and claw—watchful, waiting.

"Eric," she whispered into the dark. "Do you see me?"

"No," came his voice, ragged and earnest.

"Good. Then stay there. Wait until I call you."

"Yes, Clara."

She slipped from the bed, the cool air clinging to her nakedness like damp gauze. At the window, she opened herself, set her legs astride, whispering into the silence with the voice that was no longer wholly her own. '*Get out*'.

And out it came—her hidden twin, her unholy ward. She felt its sharp elbows, its knees, as it pained her clawing at the exit, heard it rattle out onto the wooden floor, and told it in her mind, '*Go out the window, wait on the ledge until I call you*'.

She heard its obedience, as it scraped across the floor like a spider dragging its cage of bones. She bid it to the sill and ledge outside, to cling there, unseen, grasping the cracks in the bricks and mortar while she faced the harder trial within.

The drapes fluttered, she heard it scrabbling away like a huge, hard bodied spider, no different in form other than a slight resemblance to a man merged with a woman, an 'it' in arachnid shape and temperament.

Now, the next repulsion to face, she thought, gifting her vagina to the horrific Eric. Her mind returned to him; monster in form, angel in heart. She had promised him tenderness, even as her gorge rose at the thought of his touch. His curse lay not in his soul, but in his flesh, warped by alchemy's cruelty. And she, God help her, must welcome him—body to body—if he was ever to be freed.

She slid back into the bed, pulling the covers up, though the chill of the night that had entered through the window and crept between the folds of the sheets. "Come now, Eric. My beautiful lover."

His feet were crossing the carpet, but the pat, pat of his feet upon the woven thread was like a drum beat threatening the coming of a monster. And yet, he never arrived beside her, for her to draw back the sheets, blankets and counterpane to welcome him in.

She wondered if she should call out. Had he lost heart?

His tread upon the carpet was uneven, a patter like rain before a storm. The weight of him at the foot of the bed made her breath catch. Then—oh, God—his entrance: a damp heaviness, a trail of slime against her skin. He slid up between her legs, his ruined mouth and weeping pores leaving rivulets that cooled then burned.

Revulsion surged; bile stung her throat. His scent—sweet, cloying, like lilies rotting in a crypt—threatened to undo her resolve. She nearly wept with the shame of it.

There was silence. Then his hands pressed against her waist—strangely gentle, absurdly careful. The slime that moments ago made her gag now slid like molten silk, coating her belly, her breasts. It was obscene, yet… transforming. The part of her that had recoiled found itself entranced.

Her mind began to twist upon itself, turning revulsion into ecstasy. What is this but just another form of nature? She thought wildly. Does not the spider devour her mate in the throes of coupling? Does not the bloom of the corpse flower seduce flies with the perfume of death? And what is she, if not already transformed into a creature of perversion and wonder?

Her body betrayed her then. The same slime that moments ago smothered her breath now seemed to stroke every nerve, to seep into hidden places, awakening sensations sharp and alien. A fever built in her blood. She clutched at him, not to push him away but to draw him closer.

"Eric," she gasped, not knowing if she begged him to stop or never stop.

There was a smell to him, as well, that of a body in a grave… sweet decay. She heaved in the dark, desperately trying to keep it silent.

But then his voice: "I'm making you sick, dear Clara. I should stop and leave," she heard him whisper.

"No, no." She lied. "It's the over-excitement of anticipation, the wondrous joy at the thought of your kisses, your affection, and your lust when inside me. I love your touch, your mucus is most welcome as a cooling stream on a body boiling with lust to feel that beautiful, always-erect member inside of me. Keep coming. Kiss falling upon her breasts, her mind could see the fleck of debris swimming there as his body slid up along it until a curtain of the stuff fell across her mouth, her nose, her closed eyes. It snatched her breath as she inhaled, and the curtain was drawn into her mouth and dragged down to wet her lungs.

She knew she was about to vomit, but then what was of his mouth found her gaping one, and his tongue slid inside—with it a ball of honey -textured mucus that tasted of salt.

Her revulsion gave way to sensual excitement. An odd thing, she thought, as she considered the prospect of a giant slug fucking her. The notion hooked onto something inside her mind, drew it out of a dark dungeon of depravity, a twist of nature in the way it made life in weird and exotic forms. Did the male nursery web spider enjoy the threat of being eaten by his female mate after enjoying sex with her? Did it heighten his pleasure, amplify the bliss, knowing if it failed to escape after, it would be decapitated? She thought it did, she thought she felt the same kind of high surge of excitement now, mating with Eric, knowing his look—that his revolting snot was covering her body, from his face exuding a substance so extraordinarily slimy—was the working of organic design, a joy in playing with living cells; the discovery of exploring novelty and the realisation of new sensations, of creating electrical pulses down different nerve paths, and lighting up new areas of the brain. Her brain. Her repulsion twisted into a welcome path, like that of a lost lamb to find its way back home, and her way to be drawn into a new kind of comforting conclusion.

What was a moment ago, utter revulsion, was now highly erotic. She welcomed it, wanted more of his nose's expulsion on her, over her, making her racing heart pound in her ears, causing her vagina to flood. She put her arms around him as he slid away back down her body, moving effortlessly, like rain on the surface of a clean pane of glass.

She nearly came right there and then, as his lipless mouth and nose-less face, began a wet encounter with her clitoral region, putting down layer after layer of goo and then slicking his tongue over it without friction; it was utterly sensuous, she thought, to feel—like the way ice cream melted on the tongue, or an oyster slipped down a throat… effortlessly.

"Enter me," she whispered.

In a moment, he had slid up the entire length of her body, and his rod slid into her, as a master swordsman slides his sword into its sheath. He moved up and down on her, his whole body remaining in contact with hers. There was no annoying rubbing, no bruising, or heavy weight; he all but floated on her, up and down, frictionless, gliding the surface of her oil-coated body. She loved the sound it made: shlick… shlick… shlick…

"Faster, my darling, Eric. Let yourself go—"

He did.

What was a slow burn became a race, a sprint into bliss, and she ran with him, their bodies writhing together, mindless, all care, thoughts of the world and their paths, journeys, and stories in it—discarded; there was only this moment in time. No future or past existed; two had become one. And then the explosion within her, and Eric crying out like a wounded beast, his exclamation of intense pleasure singing out, and melting into her own voice as her body rippled, and her muscles danced to the dopamine coursing in her veins, and as her mind flew out through the window and waltzed with the stars.

And when at last the fever broke, when the final shudder of release tore from her throat like a cry from the gallows, she knew something in her had changed.

Eric collapsed beside her, whimpering as though in relief, or awe, or both.

Clara lay trembling, her skin slick, her breath ragged. The moonlight found a chink in the drapes, threw silver in, caught the sheen of slime across her breasts and belly, and for a moment she thought herself some strange statue of marble and pearl.

She turned her head toward him. His face, ruined though it was, seemed softer now in the light. A weight had lifted from it, however slightly.

She had done it. She had given herself to the grotesque, and in the act, she had begun his redemption.

But in her belly, low and coiled, another thought whispered:

And what of my own? Who now will redeem me?

Clara lay in the damp heat of what had just passed, her chest rising and falling as though she had outrun death itself. The sheets beneath her clung with sweat and Eric's secretions, the perfume of decay filling her nostrils, and yet—God help her—it no longer repulsed. It exhilarated.

Beside her, Eric trembled. His twisted frame glistened like something newly hatched from a chrysalis, eyes wide and uncertain. "You should hate me," he whispered. "You should drive me back into shadow."

Clara turned, pressing a hand to the ruin of his face. Her palm slid against the slickness of his skin, and instead of recoil, she felt hunger. Hunger not of the belly, but of the soul.

"Hate?" she said softly. "No, Eric. You are the truth others would cover with silk and perfume. But I... I see the beauty in the rot."

His breath caught, ragged, as though she had not dared believe her own words. But she did. The horror of him had become the alchemy of her own release, burning away the last shreds of the shame she carried.

As she stroked his face, it felt drier; it was as though it were repairing.

"I'll go. I'll come again when your loving with me has done the miracle of restoration. I hope, Clara, I can one day save you from his evil for the beautiful gift you've just given to me."

And then he was gone. She heard the click of the mirror opening, and then the almost silent sound of it closing, and she was alone again, his seed inside her.

And from the window, she thought she heard a scuff of claw on stone.

She had left the thing outside, she recalled.

But the sound was an echo, something heard minutes before, one that in the shared bliss with Eric, she had not registered.

She threw off the coverings, wondering why she was bringing it back instead of prising its hands from the bricks of the house it clung to. She had chosen to accept or deny. Now, she was stuck with it, like a body needing its lung.

"*Return.*" She called out in a sharp whisper.

She opened her legs, but it never came. There was only silence and the faint, distant sound of a bat wing settling on the mushroom-shaped yew tree.

The stranger...

She wanted to go to the window—wanted to see what her mind was playing through, to see if it was true—the pictures conjuring from out of the doctor's potions in her body, his meddling, trying to transform her. Could she see the past...

...the winged man, descending, swooping out of the night as a cloud passed over the moon—a desperate attempt outside the window, as she gave voice and screamed out in overwhelming bliss—as it gripped, not just the cracks in the bricks and mortar, but its final hold on life...

...as *his* hands, a creature comfortable in the air without the need for purchase, prised bone and skin away, and watched it fall like a dry and brittle branch of a tree joined with a fan of leafless twigs, as it shattered on the ground beneath, three stories down.

Had he done it for her?

She was rid of it. She knew. Her altered state told her... the same way it informed her that Eric's seed had encountered an egg, freshly released from her ovary, and had blessed it with life.

Such a day... she thought as the weariness of living it stole her away.

She finally gave in to its calling, letting its comforting arms bless and guide her into a dreamless sleep.

Clara woke mid-morning to an empty house where only ghosts, long departed, dared to tread, except deep in the basement, where another young woman stirred, naked and shivering in in a dark cell lit only by a dim gaslight. Clara's half-transformed body with its heightened senses could smell her, the fishy smell of the Thames from the bucket, the young captive's only toilet in the corner of her cell.

Memory of the previous day flew into Clara's mind, a tint bird carrying a huge meal in its beak, that of memory, most grotesque and bitter sweet: the devil using the rescued girl as a sexual trampoline; the saving of Maggie and the terrible bloody torment of resisting temptation; and then Eric, the angel with the face of a Gargoyle and her sexual dance with him which had shifted from a swim in a swamp to a flight amongst angels.

She was tempted to drift back to sleep, but her still-unhardened heart would not allow it. Veyl was still out, feeding among the unsuspecting. It was an opportunity to take comfort to a soul, lost and crying in a prison of cold stone and even colder, harsh iron. She got out of bed, drew back the drapes and sucked in the fresh perfumed air. It was as she exhaled that she recalled a noise, the releasing of fingernails previously gripping brick and mortar. She lowered her head to look down below. A heap lay there, broken and scattered, like a bag of discarded bones—'it'.

She put on a flimsy nightdress—one of fine lace but little material. Its lightness of weight was welcome as she wandered out of the bedroom into an empty house.

Carrying food from the kitchen, cheese and bread, she descended the flight of stairs and through into the narrow passage with a damp brick wall on one side and a row of cells and metal grills. She was in the second one, easily found by following the odour of fish and ammonia. Clara gripped the grill, but it was locked tight. She searched along the wall on the other side and found it there—a metal ring hanging with keys. She fetched, trying them one after the other, in the lock of the grilled door until one worked, and with a click, she could pull it open.

The young woman, naked and bleeding onto her thighs, shivered as the rusty metal door whined on its pivot hinges when Clara went in.

"It's okay, I brought you food. He's not in." She said softly to the pitiful creature, curled up defensively on top of the metal springs of a bed. She sat up and stared at Clara, who saw in the dim light, them, marks the springs had made on the young woman's flesh—deep cuts down her front; he had turned her then, to intrude on her in the most obscene way, she thought.

"You were with him when I was taken here..." she voiced with hatred.

"I'm sorry. I did know he intended this. I thought him a doctor, helping people, not a monster who would do what he did to you. Did he bite you?"

She shook her head.

"Eat some of this," Clara told her with kind, soft words. She sat down next to her on the springs that cut into her gown and offered the cheese and bread. The young woman grabbed them and bit urgently into the cheese. "Thank you."

Clara studied her, the lovely young face now baring old, haunted eyes, her young, firm breasts now scarred by nails like talons, the fresh blood trickling down her thighs. Clara wondered if Veyl might have potions to ease the girl's suffering on the bookcase lined with glass bottles filled with liquids, but dare she risk a visit to the surgery upstairs?

The smell of the girl assailed her senses, which were suddenly overwhelmed, just one—the iron of blood, and a hunger deep inside of her at the smell, so strong, she could taste its sweet metal on her tongue. It caused her to salivate and ramped up the pump in her chest. Her mind was caught by the teeth of the girl as they drove into the cheese, like a wolf into a lamb. The wretched girl was in easy grasp, her hair swept back clear of her throat, so vulnerable, so easy and quick to feast there.

Clara could not believe her body's response to these stimuli. As soon as she realised her leaning forward was not the act of a human wanting to embrace another in empathy of their misery, but that of a ravenous, greedy, heartless beast—she fought against it, trying to stop its awful consequence... and lost... as her mouth seized the girl's throat, and long dog teeth pierced that rich artery, and released iron and copper, in a rich, warm, red milk, freeing it from the collagen sleeve, so it could be pumped not through the girl's body, but directly into Clara's waiting stomach, rapidly filling it with soothing balm. She felt that quivering hand let go of cheese, heard urine splashing on the cell floor, felt the ice claw of fear and terror gripping the girl's soul; her thoughts of death, of betrayal, her utter disbelief that it was happening to her. Her thoughts were not waking ones for long, as she slipped unconscious, became a limp, rag doll in Clara's welcoming hands; she could enjoy her feeding now without the nuisance of struggling, and she sucked and sucked until the glow began to dwindle and the young woman's body felt cool. Clara dropped her and lifted her head, closing her eyes and savouring the last mouthful of blood before swallowing.

She waited for her dog teeth to retract before calmly wiping her mouth and looking down at the white ghost of a woman on the metal springs. She felt no pity, despite knowing she should. Does one care for a lettuce pulled from the ground—sliced and eaten, or an apple, plucked from a tree—and bitten into? No. Why then feel sorrow for a bag of worthless seawater holding but a single life, now, all taken?

She was in the garden, delighting at the warm sun and the slight breeze on her face. Clara had relocked the door and left the weakened wretch lying there, beside the half-eaten cheese, and the blood-soaked bread—all but forgotten, bad dreams should be, for that, thought Clara must be what it was… a bad dream. She had no heart for such an act and had convinced herself quickly of such a reality.

A butterfly landed in error, briefly on Clara's rosy cheek, its gentle touch and its fragile fluttering, finding a place of loving in Clara's heart. As it took off, there was another fluttering behind her. She turned to see two black wings folding away into a dark cloak. It was him, the young, handsome man she had spoken with before.

The Wrath Of Veyl

Chapter 11: The Wrath Of Veyl

"Was it you?" she asked, pointing to the heap of bones that lay on the ground beneath her bedroom window

"I but went to shake his hand," he said with a smile on his face.

"What's your name?" She asked.

"Falcon," he replied.

"No, your real name?"

"Discarded, when transformed, so as not to dishonour my parents. I'm just Falcon now, Clara."

"What are you?"

"I'm a vampire, like Veyl."

"They're a myth."

"Are they now?" He suddenly sniffed the air. "Are you not full of someone else's metal?"

"What do you mean?"

He sniffed again. "Yes, I'm sure now, and of the Thames."

"What you smell is bad dreams."

"I was the same, in denial, when I fed from the throats of others." He told her.

"Vampires can't walk in daylight," she said.

"Now, that's a myth. We can, but the sun feels hotter, and too long gives sunburn too fast."

"Come sit under the Taxas Bacatta with me, and we'll talk in the shade. Your skin is far too pale to stay in the sun too long, and you are still in a fragile dress.; no protection from the heat of the sun."

"The Taxas Ba...?"

"It's the scientific name for the Yew tree."

"Clever. Not a peasant boy, then"

"Nor you a peasant girl, either, I sense."

He sat with his back resting against the Yew. She joined him.

"So, who did you steal the life of?" He asked.

"In my dream, a young woman, Veyl keeps in the cellar and defiles violently."

"You drank your fill. In your dream?"

"I did."

"And, the girl?"

"Sleeping it off."

"Show me"

Clara laughed. "If you climb in through my ear, there may be some fragments in my subconscious you can explore."

"I see. In the cellar, you say?"

Clara nodded and then was startled, her heart jumping to her mouth, as he unwrapped his wings, flapped once, and was so fast that only the shadow of a large bat rushed across the garden and was gone.

She wondered why. Had she frightened him off—such talk of blood sucking, and nightmares. Did he think her insane? She had forgotten something. The garlic. She put hr hand in her pocket, fetched out a bulb and peeled off three cloves, her fine, sharp nails, peeling the fabric skin from them. She crushed them in her mouth with her teeth and swallowed.

Instantly, she felt sick and fought to stave off vomiting. It settled. Had Maggie tricked her? Never before had she reacted that way to garlic. Wasn't Chicken Kiev her favourite meal? Odd!

There was a flapping sound, and Falcon landed beside, putting his wings away. "I found her."

He had red streaks down from the corners of his mouth. She pointed, "Are you bleeding?"

He felt then with his little finger, "Oops. Messy. Sorry." And wiped them away.

"You left her with blood still in her. A bad mistake. Always empty them."

"What? Was she there?"

"Yes. Dead and cold now. No more suffering for her at the devil's hands."

"You think I'm a vampire?"

"Were you bitten?"

"I was scratched by a woman who wanted to fight me."

He took her chin gently in his hand. "Let me see."

She liked his touch. It excited her. He studied her throat. "They're feint, but, yes, she drank from you. I am certain you are." He sniffed. "Have you eaten garlic?"

She nodded.

"Good. It means he can't fully transform you. Only I can do that, but only after twenty-four hours of you not eating it."

"Why would I ask you to transform me?"

He looked sad. "I'm sorry, Clara, but you'll see."

He took off.

She was alone again.

She shivered slightly. Had she been turned into a vampire? Her dreams... not dreams. How could this all have come about?

She felt oddly tired and queasy. Had the garlic upset her? Maggie's voice echoed in her mind... *"The first time you take it is like being poisoned. Likely, you'll be sick and fall asleep. But after, it won't happen again."*

It echoed over and over again as she fell into sleep, and she dreamed.

The world of the garden dissolved, as though mist had crept in through the hedges and pulled her elsewhere.

She was a child again, her shoes clicking on polished marble floors, sunlight streaming in long panes through tall sash windows. A maid hurried after her with ribbons in hand, scolding softly, but laughter bubbled from Clara's lips as she darted away. Roses bloomed outside, tended by gardeners who tipped their hats as she passed, the scent rich and indulgent.

Her father's voice came next, stern yet not unkind, calling her back to her books. The library—she remembered it so well. Walls crowded with leather-bound volumes, dust motes dancing in golden shafts of light, the faint crackle of the fire. She would curl in the deep chair, skirts spilling, dreaming of far-off lands as her governess corrected her posture.

The dream turned again, a shimmer, a tearing of edges. She saw her mother's pearls glitter at a dinner table, candlelight mirrored in polished silver. Gentlemen bowed, ladies whispered, her place secure among them, the daughter of a house in Bloomsbury.

And yet—the pearls slipped from her mother's throat, scattering across the floor. Darkness intruded, cold air sweeping the corridors. One by one, the lights in the tall house extinguished, leaving only echoes. The great doors slammed shut, and when she tried to open them again, she was thrust into narrow alleys choked with smoke and ash.

The gowns were gone. Her feet were bare. The perfume of roses had soured into the stench of sewage and coal. Faces turned toward her—not the polished, smiling faces of diners in salons, but hollow-eyed, hungry children, gaunt men sprawled drunk against brick walls, women with tired mouths and blood on their sleeves.

Clara stumbled through them, the hem of her dress now rags, clutching at the cold stone walls as voices jeered. She searched for her house, her family, her name—but the city swallowed them all, dragging her into its underbelly.

A hand caught hers. For a moment, she thought it was her mother's, soft and jewelled—but no, it was a beggar's claw, skeletal, dragging her down to where the light did not reach.

She cried out, but the dream sealed her throat. The great house in Bloomsbury, the gardens, the laughter, all dissolved into shadow. And she was left with the sick knowledge that she had once been someone— and had become but a forgotten waif of the East End.

The dream began sweet, a golden memory.

She was in Bloomsbury again, her hair brushed smooth by a maid as she gazed out of her bedroom window. Below, carriages rattled over clean cobblestones. Her father's voice carried from the study, rich with command, while her mother's pearls glimmered in the firelight at supper. Laughter, music, the clink of silver spoons—her world had once been secure, perfumed, and untouched by want.

But the music faltered. The dream tilted.

At the far end of the table, a man sat where no man should be, his features lost in shadow though the candles burned bright. He raised a glass—wine, no, not wine, something darker—and though no one else seemed to see him, Clara felt his eyes upon her. Her laughter withered in her throat.

She blinked, and the table was gone. She was in the library again, the fire guttering low. Books slipped from the shelves like corpses from their coffins. A whisper ran along the spines, hissing her name. And in the far corner—again—he stood. The same figure, tall, elegant, indistinct, yet somehow inevitable.

"Veyl…" she tried to say, but the dream stole her voice.

Then came the street. The grand doors of the Bloomsbury house slammed shut, leaving her outside in the fog. She pounded on the panels, but they would not open. Her silks had vanished, her feet bare upon the grime. Hunger gnawed her belly, and cold sank into her bones. Around her, the alleyways unfolded—smoke, gin, bodies in heaps. The East End had swallowed her whole.

Yet still he lingered. She saw him on a rooftop, cloak drifting like smoke, watching. When she begged for help, he turned away. When she tried to flee, he was already there, ahead of her. She began to wonder if he had led her, step by step, from one life to another, stripping her of name, fortune, memory.

The dream cracked further. She was stumbling among shadows, the scent of roses curdling to blood. Every turn she took, he was near, unseen yet present. A hand on her shoulder, cold and possessive. A voice—silken, cruel—whispered: You were never yours to keep.

She screamed, but only bats took flight from the rafters above, their wings blotting out the moon.

The dream grew heavier, like a velvet curtain falling.

Clara was running now—bare feet over cobbles slick with rain, her breath tearing her throat raw. The city twisted around her, its streets no longer her London, but something older, darker. Lamps bled light instead of casting it. Windows blinked shut as she passed, as if all eyes turned away from her.

She stumbled, fell, and the stones beneath her rippled, warm, wet. Blood seeped between them, spreading out in a slow tide, staining her hands, her gown, her lips. She gagged at the taste, yet some part of her—horrifying, unfamiliar—wanted more.

Above, the night erupted with wings. Not birds, not bats—shapes too large, too human. They wheeled and swooped in silence, and from their midst, one form descended. Cloaked. Waiting. Watching. His face was hidden, yet she knew him. She had always known him.

Veyl!

His name roared inside her skull, though no lips moved. The shadows pressed close, suffocating, and then she was not running anymore. She was in a chamber of stone, candlelight flickering, the air heavy with incense and iron. He was beside her, impossibly close, a hand at her throat.

"Mine," the whisper came. A single word, yet it drowned the chamber, it filled her bones.

And then the teeth. White, sharp, glinting. She felt them at her skin—not piercing yet, but hovering, threatening, inevitable. The promise of ecstasy, the sentence of death. Her body arched, torn between terror and a pull she could not resist.

She tried to wake, but the dream held her fast. Memories of Bloomsbury scattered like ash. Only the hunger remained, gnawing, endless.

And in the haze of her dream, she realised: she had not fallen from wealth to ruin by mischance. She had been led. Each step, each loss, orchestrated. Not fate, but his will.

The shadow of Veyl was her undoing—perhaps her rebirth.

The dream clenched tighter, and Clara realised there was no waking—only falling.

She stood once more in her family's drawing room in Bloomsbury. Chandeliers glittered, fine China shone, music drifted from the grand piano where her mother's fingers danced across the keys. The warmth of home should have comforted her, but the room was wrong. Too silent between notes. Too cold in the corners. Her father sat in his chair by the fire, but his eyes were empty pits, coals smouldering within. Her mother's smile was stretched too wide, frozen, as though carved in wax.

The guests at the party turned their heads all at once, every face pallid and slack-jawed, every gaze fixed on Clara. They rose, moving in unison, and she stepped back. Their mouths opened, not in greeting, but in a silent howl. From within, something gleamed—fangs, wet and glistening.

Her heart thudded, but the sound echoed like a drum, reverberating through the chamber until it no longer belonged to her at all. She clutched at her chest—her heartbeat was being stolen, drained into the shadows that writhed behind the velvet curtains.

And there he was again. Veyl. No longer cloaked, but vast, towering, his presence filling every corner. His wings unfurled, blotting out the chandelier light, casting the party into darkness. He raised a hand, and all the guests fell to their knees, their lifeless faces turned toward him like flowers to the sun.

Clara wanted to scream, to run, but her feet were rooted in place. The velvet beneath her slippers had turned to soil, damp and loamy. Roots of the yew tree coiled up from below, snaring her ankles, drawing her down. She struggled, but the more she fought, the deeper she sank, earth filling her mouth, her lungs, her eyes—until she could see nothing but the dark between roots.

Yet even there, even smothered, she felt him. The whisper. It seared into her mind—an angry voice. "Clara!"

She woke with a start, thankful to have escaped her dream.

And there he was in front of her.

"What have you done?"

He was shouting. "Where the fuck is Maggie? Why did you take the life of my plaything?"

Questions, questions.

"Wait!" she shouted back. "Let me collect my thoughts."

He leaned forward—a darker shadow cast over her than that of the yew tree. She watched him.

"You reek of garlic. Is this Maggie's doing?"

She knew not how to reply.

"My maid gone. My sex toy dead. Well, young lady, since you rebel against my teaching, until you've learnt your lesson, you have a new role. Not one, but two. No longer will you be my apprentice learning the art to be strong in your new form; you'll act as my maid, and my wretched woman from the Thames. *Get up. Go and make us breakfast, even though it's already midday*."

He had used the voice on her. But she had the voice, too. *"No!"*

She never even saw his open hand move. It hit the side of her face the way a swatter flattens a fly crawling across a table.

She was swept to the ground, and at his mercy as the fragile garment she wore was ripped from her body, and tossed aside. She saw him reach up and break a bough, felt the sting of the leaves thrashing her body, stinging, cutting the surface of her skin.

He stopped. "*Never try the voice on me. Find Maggie's outfit and serve me breakfast."*

She felt foolish. Dressed the way Maggie did, and put two plates down on the table to serve food onto them.

"Good," he said, now curtsy.

She did. He pointed. "Sit there, eat, and don't dare talk until I'm less angry with you."

She ate in silence. When they had finished, he spoke softly. "Clean up here, and meet me in my laboratory. Change your maid's dress, and wear your nightdress, the fragile one that's flimsy. Come like that and barefoot. If you disobey me, just once, after you've meddled around without my guidance and instruction, then despite my reluctance to cause you pain, I'll cause you such distress, you'll wish yourself as dead as the hapless wretch whose life you took."

Clara opened her mouth to say something, "Bu…"

"Don't speak. Be silent. When I want you to talk again, I'll tell you."

She began clearing up, feeling his eyes watching her every move.

She had cleared up, washed and dried the dishes, and was not removing her maid's dress and slipping on the fragile nightdress. Her heart was full of fear and trepidation at why he wanted her this way. She'd never seen him so angry with her. Was he going to rape her? Would such violence on her body as she witnessed him dish out to the woman in the basement damage her, or worse, the life starting within her?

She went to the mirror, wondering if Eric and Maggie were watching her from behind. There was nothing either of them could do to help, nor, it seems, the winged man called Falcon. She was on her own. Her hand trembled as she pulled down the dress, went to the door, and opened it.

The hallway seemed dark, like a passage where the gaslights dimmed in reverence to a prisoner leaving his cell to be led, screaming and kicking, to the rope that would hang him. Was she walking towards her own execution? The air stifled her. It drifted up from below as she descended the stairs, an atmosphere that reeked of rotten eggs, gunpowder smoke, and death.

The surgery was busy with several Bunsen burners on high, below bubbling liquids in several glass holders. Small clouds rose from one large phial that boiled fast and was extremely agitated. He was at the bench and looked up briefly to point before returning to his endeavours.

She looked to where he'd pointed, and her legs turned to jelly. She took faltering step after another and went to a harsh-looking, high-backed metal chair, with its rough leather straps, and iron bracelets attached to its legs. She sat down on the cold metal seat, her mind drifting in the iron of its construction. It was a thing of pain and torture. It screamed out to her with the voices of those who had sat in it before her, wretches who'd witnessed the stuff of their nightmares transforming into physical form, terrible and soul-destroying. Oh, how they had protested and shouted, begged, pleaded, offered their mothers and children as sacrifice to try and stop the pain, but the agony did not stop, the straps and torture continued, relentless, until they went mad.

He spoke without looking up, his voice soft and purring. "A lot of guests have sat in that chair... patients too, and sometimes, just someone I had taken a dislike to, or had offended me. It has many purposes but just one function. Tell me what that function is, Clara.

"To restrict movement and escape," she replied, her tone trembling in tone and pitch, hoarse, the voice of a dry mouth in fear of its own words' meaning.

"Good girl. Quite right. Now, save me the labour and strap yourself into it. Tightly, mind you, so the straps bite. I'll check, and if the leather is not on the verge of cutting into you, I'll over-adjust them so they do, and you'll bleed from their bite."

She looked at them. There were so many.

"I'm uncertain which goes where and their individual purpose," she said, her voice now weaker than before."

"Don't concern yourself with their purpose. You're a clever girl, you work them out one at a time." He said, without looking up. "I'm too busy finishing a potion just for you."

She looked again at the phials, all boiling fast; the black smoke smelt of the increasingly dark atmosphere of putrid flesh, and body-snatched graves left open by thieves, and fouling the atmosphere.

She took hold of two leather straps and saw how they fastened, pressing two metal rings over her breasts, and positioned a smaller one below them and central. Next, she put her hand down and pulled a single black one with sharp iron studs lining it. Opening her legs, as it would not reach to clasp the central ring until she did. It was the worst of it, the metal studs pushed through the crack of her vagina, and as she buckled it to the ring, she realised, as the studs bit into her soft flesh through the nightdress, that it was designed to irritate, scratch, and cut into her most sensitive regions. The buckle took, and she fastened it tight until tears ran from her eyes.

"They're done," she said.

He went over. "Put your arms on the armrests."

She did. He slid metal cuffs over her wrists, anchoring them there, before bending down and putting the metal bands around her ankles. He checked everything and then said, "Good. How does it feel?"

"Terrible, painful, cruel," she said.

"I think that strap," he said, pointing, "might chafe your thighs. Your legs are too close together."

He went around to the back of the chair, and from behind he said, "Fortunately, this handle should stop that."

She heard a sound like metal teeth interlocking with other teeth, and felt a tug on each of her legs. The front metal legs of the chair began to scrape on the stone floor, dragging her legs open wider. The leather there bit tighter into her crotch, the studs finding her soft interior and piercing the tissue there. Blood seeped out and through the nightdress. The chair legs only stopped moving just before her hips threatened to dislocate.

Veyl reappeared at the front of her. "Now, a glass of water after that. I expect your mouth is dry."

He walked off out of sight and returned with a large pitcher and a glass. He poured water from it into the glass and brought it up to her mouth. "Open wide," he told her. "I promise you, it's only water."

She opened her mouth, and he carefully tipped it in, showing great patience by stopping frequently and letting her swallow before continuing. When the glass was empty, he filled it again and said, "One more glass."

She shook her head, "No, that's enough."

"I'll say when it's enough, not you. Now drink."

She drank again until that glass was empty.

"Again," he said, and forced her to drink a third.

When the glass was empty, he took it and the pitcher away, returning with a pot that had a paintbrush sticking out of it. She watched as he took the brush, loaded it with a thick gooey liquid from the pot and proceeded to brush copious amounts onto the leather strap running through her vagina and up her front to the ring between her breasts.

"What is that?" She asked.

"A concoction of mine. The straps are not of ordinary leather. They're quite special. When wetted by water, they shrink a lot. This liquid increases the effect and, in fact, allows water to run along it. The straps and the paint I'm using react better to the composition of urine. You'll see for yourself when you need to pee."

"Why are you doing this?" he asked.

"To punish you for your meddling, the minute my back is turned. A dead friend in a heap in the garden, my maid ran off, and my plaything dead in the cellar. This will ensure you never do such things again, and you'll carry out my will."

He walked to the bench and turned off all the Bunsen burners. "I'm off to place adverts for a new maid. I'll be gone for a few hours."

"Wait. Don't leave me here like this, I beg you."

He laughed. "It's to make sure you don't get into any mischief while I'm out. Tonight, you can help me carry the girl's body to the river."

The Party

Chapter 12: The Party

Within an hour, Clara become desperately wanting to wee. She feared the consequences—the straps bit hard enough already. It terrified her, the thought of those studs, already piercing the surface of her tissues, and the straps so tight across her breasts that she could hardly breathe.

She focused all her attention on stopping her bladder from opening, but still, a tiny leak started. It trickled out. She couldn't stop it, and then it became a torrent, spraying out from the sides of the belt, there, so tight against her urethra. The urine ran over her skin, down her front, underneath, and she saw it defying gravity, crawling along the painted leather up the clasp beneath her breasts. But nothing else seemed to happen. Had Veyl said all that to put fear into her and make her struggle against the need to wee?

Maybe he wasn't so bad after all, was the last thing she thought, before the strap between her legs tore into her, making her scream. It cut into her rectum, her urethra, her vagina, and then snatched at the strap up to her breasts, and pulled the ring there, until the leathers across her breasts were as tight as sprung wire. Blood was running down her body, between her legs, and onto the floor.

The pain was like nothing she'd ever known. Screaming did nothing to relieve it. The strap between her legs only stopped cutting further into her when it met the hard pubic bone. Then it pulled so tight on the ring beneath her breasts that the two rings on top of them pulled until the metal disappeared into her breasts, cutting a perfect circle in each, like a pastry cutter on soft pastry.

The door to the laboratory creaked open. Veyl walked in, his hands over his ears. God, the din you're making. I'd swear it'll wake the dead."

He walked over calmly, put his hand on the clasped claw, locking all the straps together beneath her breast and snapped it open.

The straps flew off as if they were on springs. She slumped in the chair, badly wounded and sobbing.

"Don't worry, you're half transformed. In thirty minutes, you'll not even see a scar—you'll be completely intact again. Go wash yourself after and put on some fine dresses. Be ready to go out tonight."

He left.

Miraculously, Clara discovered with great joy, that Veyl had been right. Her body repaired before her very eyes. She had washed in a cold water bath, dried, and now stared before the long mirror in her bedroom, looking at her naked body.

What could not be repaired so readily was the memory of her pain, the terror and the torture. It scarred her mind. She sensed movement before she heard the click—a sixth sense, or her heightened senses. The mirror swung open, and Maggie stepped out.

"Did he put you in his infernal torture chair?"

"He did. Have you tried it?"

"Only the threat of it. I'm sorry. Was it because of me?"

Clara shook her head. "No. All my doing. Hold on. I brought you some food."

Clara went to a bundle, a knotted sheet. "There's bread, cheese, and fruit in there. He never checks the larders, so he won't know it's gone. How's Eric?"

Maggie kissed her and took the bundle. "Eric's coming back to rights. He told me to tell you that once he's back to his former self, he wishes to come and thank you."

Clara nodded. She wondered if she should say she was pregnant with his child, but thought not to. "What do you do about toileting?"

"Ha! Difficult. Eric has removed slates from the roof and fixed a waxed sheet there to stop rain from coming in. He used wooden boxes, veg and fruit crates from the market. He's arranged them like steps. We climb, squeeze through the opening, then shit and piss down the side of the roof. When the rain comes, it carries it away down to the gutter."

"And cleaning after?"

"I don't wish to say."

"*Tell me.*" Clara used the voice on her.

"We lick each other clean."

Clara smiled at the thought of it.

"Clara. Please don't use the voice on me. I'm your friend."

Clara nodded.

"I'm to go out tonight. I know not where, but you and Eric can wash and use the house when we go. Veyl loves the night, so I don't think we'll be back early."

"Thank you. I should go. Spray perfume into the air after I close the mirror, or he'll smell my presence was here in the room."

Clara nodded, watched her go and close the mirror, then sprayed the room and herself.

After a little rest on the bed, Clara put on a fine outfit. No sooner had she stroked it down than a knock on the bedroom door, which opened immediately after.

"You look good. Now, I've forgiven you for your meddling. I trust my little punishment will have made you more compliant?"

It was Veyl.

"I made a mistake. It won't happen again."

He sniffed the air. "Did you bathe in the perfume? It lies heavy on the air."

I knocked over the bottle when I stumbled and it spilt onto the dressing table," she said. "Where are we going?"

"To the river, and then the East End, or maybe the West End. I've not decided yet."

"The body?"

"Yes. That first. My driver will do the work, but you'll watch and keep lookout. The young lass is already in my carriage, waiting for you to sit beside her."

"More punishment." She said.

"No, no… someone has to prop her up in case the carriage has to stop, and people look in."

She climbed in and sat on the red velvet next to the pale, bloodless lass she had fed upon. Was there pity in her heart? Some. Was she not hungry by change not of her design or asking? Did the desire not come from a desperate need in her subconscious that overwhelmed her

140

thoughts? The door opened, and Veyl climbed in, all smiles. "Hold onto her. When we hear the door slam shut, we'll be taking off at a gallop."

True to his word, the door slammed closed, and the carriage leapt forward. The girl fell onto Clara, startling her when her dead eyes opened and stared up at her, with her pale, cold face and bloodless lips, in a brain-dead head from her lap—accusing, questioning, glad to be out of a life which had treated her so harshly.

"Prop her up and hold her hand," Veyl said.

Clara lifted her and took her cold, icy hand into her warm one. Odd, for a moment, Clara thought she felt one of her fingers twitch.

"Who dressed her in these fresh, fine clothes?" Clara asked Veyl.

"I did. Does she not look fine? So different now to when we saw her vomiting up that eel."

"Is she really dead?"

The carriage swung, too fast, she thought, as it took a corner, and the girl fell almost into her lap again, but Clara surprised herself by grabbing her quickly and restoring her. She put an arm around her to keep her steady. Veyl watched and smiled to himself.

"I was thinking, Clara. Maybe she would make a fine new maid?"

Before she could answer, Veyl took something from his pocket, opened it, and passed it to her. She looked at it—a pocket knife.

"I found Falcon's bite on her throat, the other side of yours. She's a strong one—dead, but still blood and metal inside her. I gave her a tiny drop of mine. Open her mouth, and then open one of your veins and drop more into her."

"What? N…"

She stopped short of such a reply. There was no such thing as saying no. She slit her wrist, but not deeply, and pulled the young woman's dead mouth open, letting her metal-rich blood stream in. Veyl watched. "That's enough. Put your finger on your cut, apply pressure, and wait."

"Why am I doing this?" She asked.

"Because I need a maid."

"Because you need sex." She ventured, a statement, not a question.

"Just a maid. No excitement there with her a second time."

He knows about Falcon. How much? Could she ask? Maybe

141

another time, when she's caught up with events. "No river, then?"

He shook his head. "No need. I've decided she needs to feed, rather than swim. She's not like you. Yes, you drank from her, but you're not transformed yet. Falcon is, but still not as wise I am. His error in not taking the last drop has made her into a different thing. She is... what is the term, now... ah, yes... a kind of zombie vampire. You control her as you took most of her life. The thread still inside her can only be worked by you, sometimes me, if I use the voice on her, but not Falcon."

"Who is Falcon?" Clara asked.

"We'll talk about that young man another time, but don't be taken in by his good looks and silken tongue."

The carriage made a several turns. The young, pale woman next to Clara rolled one way and then the other, with Clara needing to right her after each movement.

The carriage slowed and ground to a halt. Clara looked out the carriage window to see a large house with a wide sweep of stairs leading up to a large double doorway. A man in a smart man-servant costume stood there, asking for the names of the many people entering through.

"Oh, look, she's back with us," Veyl said with a great deal of delight.

Clara turned her head to see the girl sitting up straight with staring, unblinking eyes, in an expressionless face.

"Tell her to go in by your side. The three of us are going in there to join a wealthy household party. I need a new plaything. I'm sure I'll find an upper-class one in there. Be sure to only take one glass of punch. Afterwards, the concoction I made today will be swimming in it, once I've tipped the phial in my pocket into the punch bowl." Veyl said.

"Walk with me, smile, stay by my side," Clara told the young woman.

Veyl got out and offered a hand to each of the other two, more for show, for the watching house servant, than genuine. They climbed the stairs. Veyl produced an invitation card, and the three of them went in. The servant at the door never noticed a fluttering in the air over the rooftops, as a handsome man in a black cloak, swooped overhead and landed on an empty balcony.

They were inside a very large room. People in fine attire mingled and chatted, glasses of punch in their hands. She stayed with the zombie-vampire, as Veyl had described her, and watched him talking to the host, a middle-aged, attractive woman by the long drinks table. He was sly; she saw how he talked for a few minutes, moved along the table, engaged another in conversation, and when he moved the phial from pocket to hand, and its contents into each punch bowl, his action was super-human, barely perceptible, it was so fast.

As he reached the end of the table, she heard a whisper, not in her ear, in her mind.

'Falcon?' she mouthed without words. 'Is that you in my head?'

'I'm upstairs', came the whisper.

'How can you talk in my mind, so?'

'I can connect to the one I desire. The emotion connects me, but only over a short distance'.

'Veyl is walking back to me. Get out of my head, please. I need to focus. It doesn't pay to displease him'.

Silence.

"Here we are. Two beautiful companions, with whom to watch the show with. Don't drink any more punch." He turned to zombie-vampire. "I expect you're hungry, dear. Don't fret. A fine meal will be yours very soon."

"What kind of show?" Clara ventured to ask.

"One to help me decide the prettiest belle, bar you two fine ladies, in the room. Remember, I'm here to select an interesting playmate. It's to spare you having to suffer such attentions from me. So, you should help because if I fail to get one that's as beautiful as you, I will be in your bed tonight and many nights after."

Clara shivered internally. Her mind drifted back to the cell in the dungeon, the shaking of the bed, the springs ringing out, and the terrible cuts they made on this poor wretch beside her, staring out of eyes that still seemed absent of life.

He wanted her to help him snatch someone from this party and do the same, if not worse, to her. Help? You bet I will, she said in her mind. I'll snatch her myself for you to use—anything to prevent me being used so.

"Where's the wretch going?" Veyl asked. It wasn't a question; it was an accusation that she, Clara, had not been keeping her close by. "Get her back, quickly, before the mindless shell bites someone."

Zombie-vampire had rapidly attracted admirers just a short distance away. They were trying to engage her in conversation. She wasn't talking, just looking, unblinking, at the front of their necks.

Fuck! Clara swept up to her, just as her head was dropping towards one of the men's necks, a male too busy looking down the top of her dress to notice.

"Annie, love. You're not to stray so far from father. Sorry, gentlemen, my sister's been poorly. This is her first night out. We still need to look after her. She's been hospitalised for many months, and she's still very fragile." Clara said, and took her away.

"Well done. She's your responsibility. If she embarrasses us or worse, I will not punish her; of course, a price needs to be paid for one's bad actions." Veyl said, smiling at her.

A ringing sound. Clara looked to see the middle-aged woman with a handbell.

"Ladies and gentlemen, please fill your glasses with the house punch and then take your glasses and clear the centre. Our tiny orchestra at the end will begin the dancing with a delightful melody, the Vienna Waltz by John Strauss. Please choose a partner and let yourselves go with gaiety and with light foot. Enjoy." The woman said.

"Well, this should be interesting," Veyl turned to Clara and said. "I think Zombie girl might enjoy a dance. Tell her, she's to dance with me."

"But neither of us has done such a dance," Clara said.

"I doubt if she has, but you most certainly have. Choose a young man when the music starts, smile at him, give it a try."

They waited until everyone collected their punch.

Clara noticed a new figure dressed in black and white drift in through the door—Falcon, just as the host rang the bell again. "Ladies and gentleman, drink your punch, put your glasses behind you against the wall. Best not to end up with bloody feet, as the waltz is best danced to without your shoes on."

Veyl sniffed the air. "Ah, I think you have a potential dancing partner. That is, if I don't go over and shoo the little birdie away."

"Will you hurt him?" She asked.

"No, no. He needs to feed, too. I'll let him join our feast tonight, just this time."

People began to move to the edge, downing their punch to give courage, Clara thought, to approach the ladies and ask for their hands, their bodies, for the waltz. It all went quiet, as the first notes drawn out of the cosmos by Strauss, echoed and connected with the soul inside Clara—a beautiful stirring of memories; another life before the back streets and alleys—the music, images of mother and father, caring, Christmases filled with toys and surprises.

"May I have the pleasure of your hand with mine on the floor, Clara?"

Falcon... his hand outstretched. She turned to see if Veyl approved, only to see him stepping onto the dance floor with Zombie. Clara took his hand. Immediately, her feet, her body, remembered the steps. She spun with him, moved in a circle beside other couples in a graceful, joyful dance; John Straus had created something timeless, a capture of the rapture of being alive, young, and excited at its potential.

Oh, how she danced, but she was no longer dancing there at that party, but at another one, the one at her home in Bloomsbury. Memories were flooding into her mind. Her blood was pumping, not just with copper and iron, but with silk and cotton, soft smells of fine perfume, of lace and finery. A man, masked. Of course, it was Halloween. Her parents had held a masked ball, their huge living room transformed into a themed dance hall. All her friends and neighbours had been invited, and no one knew who was behind their masks. It was all part of the theme, a celebration of something... what... who?

"He was there," she heard Falcon say, his arms around her now as she broke from memory and looked around her. The other dancers were casting off their clothes as they danced. The waltz music reached its end but never stopped—starting over again with more tempo as everyone tore off their garments, ripping them from their own bodies or others dancing close by, driven by something dark, something that once bubbled in glass phials and tubes, and now frothing in dancers, maddened with lust—the dancing, lost souls in the room.

Da, da, dum, da-dum, da-dum, d-dum, da—

　　　　the music went.

A blouse… a bodice… a shirt… torn with each twirl and step.

Da, da, dum, da-dum, da-dum, d-dum, da—

　　　　the music went.

Naked bodies, copulating whilst standing and laughing, pulsating, and Veyl, there in the middle, calm, watching all, unmoving, and zombie woman beside him, her mouth at the neck of a young buck, sucking the metal in his veins from him, unblinking eyes and greedy mouth, turning his rosy-cheek, young face into titanium white.

Clara stopped dancing and just stared.

"He's done this many times. Once, he carried you from such a party. You managed to escape, but seeing what happened that night left you bereft of thought and memory." Falcon said.

She was confused.

"I have to leave you, Clara. I need to feed."

She turned to ask questions, but he was no longer there; he was at the neck of a middle-aged woman, naked in his arms—the host.

A light touch on her shoulder. She turned.

"I have her. Collect zombie, and you two will help me carry her to my carriage outside." Veyl told her.

A young, beautiful and slender woman lay against him as he cuddled her. She looked half asleep, like she was sleepwalking. Clara was bewildered. Everything had happened so fast.

"*Do it! Think later*," Veyl said.

The voice. He used it on her. Why did he need to do that, she wondered? She went and pulled zombie from the man, but smelt iron, and something moved inside her, something dark that took her mind, as her own teeth came out, and her mouth fell upon zombie's meal, only to steal precious metals of iron and copper, not wasted and still, within the pipelines of a young, near-dead man. She emptied him, pushed zombie-girl towards Veyl, and said, "Help him with that woman. Do it now."

The red velvet felt comforting to her as the carriage took off. Clara, Zombie-woman and Veyl had left the party with a young woman held up between them as if she had drunk too much, still entranced by Veyl using the voice on her, down the steps into the waiting coach. The door servant was seemingly too entranced and busy in his attentions towards another female servant to notice that the stolen woman wore only her undergarments.

She now sat between Clara and zombie-woman, eyes closed, seemingly unaware.

"There's a slim chance she may come out of the slumber I've caused to her, panic, and leap out. We should watch over her closely until we're home safe and sound." Veyl told Clara. "It happened just once before."

He paused, had an odd look about him, Clara noticed.

"It took me some time to find her, lost and hungry, and to collect her, not leave her so lost. She was the most beautiful of all I've taken. I believe I loved her. How could I possibly desert her?

He's talking about me, she realised. Me!

A Policeman Calls

Chapter 13: A Policeman Calls

The carriage pulled up outside Veyl's house.

"Walk her into the house between yourself and zombie-girl in case our neighbours are watching through their netted windows," Veyl said.

"I've renamed her, Annie," Clara told him.

He laughed. "Okay, fine. Take the keys. I'll be in just after."

He got out and spoke to the driver while Clara and Annie guided the half-asleep young woman, wearing only her underwear, into the house. "Take her in here," Clara said, pointing at the door to the kitchen.

They sat her in a wooden chair at the table.

'Good. Now, Annie, go and take that dress off and put on the maid's uniform and come back here. Don't tarry.'

Annie walked out at Veyl's command. He sat at the table, looking at the new woman. "Isn't she beautiful. Eighteen years old, and with a lovely name. She's the youngest daughter of our party host."

"What's her name?" Clara asked.

"Ruth," Veyl said.

"Do you intend to keep her in that awful dungeon?"

He smiled that smile which always made Clara shiver inside. "No. She's to share your room and that large, soft four-poster bed."

Clara didn't like it, but she knew better than to utter a single word in protest. "How will you stop her from running off?" She asked. "Will you drug her or use the voice?"

"No. You'll see. It's the best method of all. She keeps her free will, her mind intact, and she'll begin a normal life here with us. A beautiful addition... a sister for you. Don't bite her. And make sure zombie Annie doesn't bite her, or it'll be the chair for you and more."

"Are you going to use her for sex?" Clara risked asking.

"Certainly. That's why I took her. You'll be able to watch as it will be in your bed. The reason is so that I can look at your lovely face while I pound into her soft, tight interior, and imagine I'm really inside you."

Clara shivered visibly.

"Are you cold?" He asked,

"A little," She lied.

"Let me wake her up. You're going to love this. Help me take her to my laboratory. I wouldn't want her falling down the stairs."

Clara watched as he tightened the last strap. Ruth was in the metal chair. Veyl straightened and checked his handiwork. "There, a bit tighter than you're starting position," he said. He walked around to the front of the chair. He turned briefly to look at Clara. "This is the first step of controlling her."

He twisted back to the girl, ***"Wake up!"***

Ruth stirred. Her eyes opened. She looked around, down at herself, and struggled, her mouth protesting. "Where am I. Let me go!"

Veyl slapped her face so hard, Clara thought Ruth's head would fly off.

"Quiet!"

She sobbed.

Clara watched her paleface glowing red one side.

"I need you to listen. I'm Veyl. You recall me talking to you and your mother? Don't speak. Nod your head if you do."

"I d…"

Slap!

The sound of his hand against her already-stinging face echoed around the room.

"Each time you utter a sound. I'll strike your face again." Veyl said. "Now answer my question."

Ruth sobbed more, tears streaming down her face, as she nodded in silence.

"Good. That's better. Let me get you some cool water. I expect your mouth is dry through fear. Am I right?"

The young woman nodded.

He walked off, returned, and as he her gave her two glasses of water, then drew up a chair in front of her.

"Don't dare speak, unless I ask you too. Now, I've kidnapped you to be my companion. You must never disobey me. My first instruction is, you must not attempt to leave this house. I know that no matter what you promise me now, that you will. Which would mean I'd catch you.

And then I would whip you with cat-o'-nine-tails to within an inch of your life. Your body will be scarred until the day to die. To avoid that, and leave it as a threat, I'm punishing you now for an escape attempt."

"But I haven't tr…"

"Slap, slap!"

She burst out crying.

"I told you not to speak. Did I not?"

"You d…"

Slap!

"Each time you speak without me asking you to, I'll give you another of those. Do you understand?"

Ruth nodded.

Clara felt pity for her.

"You wonder why I want you as my companion, don't you?" Veyl told her.

Ruth nodded.

"I intend to have you like a wife. I will fuck you silly whenever I wish. If you lift even a little finger to resist me, I'll give you a night or two back in this chair. You will also help Annie, the maid, and be a loving sister to Clara here, just behind me. She will treat you kindly, and so will I once you've become compliant."

He stood up.

"Come on, Clara. It's late. We'll return in the morning. Be sure to close your bedroom door tight, or her screams will surely wake you."

It'd been a long day, and she was so tired. Had she really taken the last drop of blood from the person Annie had bitten? She found it difficult to believe she'd done such a thing. Then it began, far away, the muted screams of that pure young lass in the lab in his infernal chair. Clara thought her a virgin. Was that why Veyl had chosen her? Did he prefer them to bleed on his first penetration, to feel first pain and forever put his face and name to it?

The screams grew louder, urgent—the one sound in all of humanity that made any human wish to go and rescue or kill the sufferer. Clara knew she could not go, or once he found out, it would be her pissing, screaming, and wishing for death.

She turned over and put the pillows over her ear.

Morning came. She woke. There were no more screams, but there was a tap on her door. It opened, Annie stood there, and mumbled something unclear.

"Again," Clara said.

"Mas.. t.. er, he… um… he… ask me… ge… t."

"He wants me? Where? In the lab?"

Annie nodded.

She went, still wearing her nightdress. Zombie-Annie, slower moving, eyes unblinking, followed her down the stairs and passages. Clara arrived at the metal door and found it wide open.

"Come in, Clara." She heard Veyl say from inside. "She's asleep."

Clara went in and walked over to see poor Ruth, the straps cutting deeply into her body, the rings no longer visible.

Veyl turned.

Clara could smell metal; the blood from Ruth's body soaked into her white underwear, turning it scarlet. Do I feel sorry for her? Clara asked herself. She crept closer, her eyes fixed only on Ruth's tender throat. It was irresistible, like approaching the final moments before an orgasm… the point where you're about to feel your body surrender to the chemistry built into you, the no-return to thought until it was done.

She felt her teeth extending, pushing through her gums, forcing her jaws to back-slip and tighten her lips out of the way. She positioned herself ready to grab that sleeping prey and draw its life into her veins.

Veyl felt her presence, her lust in the aroma from her body.

"Stop!"

She froze.

"You will not bite her, not now, not ever. Learn control over your lust. Do not let your animal mind take over your cunning brain." Veyl said, using the voice.

Her teeth retracted, her mind cleared.

"Sorry. It was an automatic reaction." She said. "She's badly wounded. You left her too long in the chair. She's split in two down there," she pointed at Ruth's groin. "And those rings, pulled deep into her breasts are cracking her ribs. Her life appears already forfeit. I was simply going to take her metal while it remained fresh." Clara said, with knowledge, which she sensed as being right.

"It seems the concentration of uric acid and creatinine in her urine is more than yours and others who've sat in that chair. Had I known, I would not have left her so long." Veyl said. "But never mind. Take this. Tell zombie-Annie to help you make hot water and prepare a bath for her."

He passed a large glass bowl-like container with a neck and a cork stopper to her.

"She has enough life left in her to obey the voice. Set the bath in the kitchen, and I'll tell her to go there." Veyl said. "Put the potion in the water and ensure she stays immersed in the bath until she shivers with the water being cold. Dry her, take her to your bed, hug her and do not let go of her until she wishes to rise. Do it right, and she'll restore."

"But..."

"But nothing. She's not a meal. I made a misjudgement with the lesson. Treat her kindly. I'll leave now and bring you back metal to feed on."

It was late afternoon. Clara helped Ruth out of the bath to dry her and saw the miracle working on the potion she'd put into the water. Her wounds were visibly healing.

Ruth had not spoken a single word, just letting out moans and groans, as Clara gently bathed her. Even whilst drying her, she uttered no sound. Clara began to wonder if bearing so much pain and torment had stolen Ruth's mind. She finished drying her, and with her still naked, guided and helped her up the stairs to her bedroom, where she guided her into bed.

Clara took off her nightdress, got into bed beside Ruth, and cuddled into her, wrapping her arms around her body and stroking the back of her head. "You're safe now, my dear sister. No more pain for you. Sleep. Feel my warmth and let it soothe you."

"Why?" She heard Ruth croak.

"Why, what? The torture?"

Ruth shook her head. "Why was I taken?"

"He told you. Did he not tell you? He wants you as a sex toy and a companion."

"Will you help me escape?" Ruth asked.

"Are you mad? Have you not suffered enough? You have no idea what he will do to you if you try or even think such a thing. Forget it."

"They'll find me. My father's high up in the government. He won't rest until I'm found. He'll get the police onto it."

"Take this opportunity to rest. Let your wounds heal and enjoy this moment of safety." Clara said.

Ruth went quiet and closed her eyes. A short time later, they were both asleep.

Clara only woke when she heard the doorbell ringing. Someone outside was pulling the cord, which made it clang away in the lower hall. She jumped out of bed, grabbed her nightdress, and went out into the hall. She heard Veyl's voice. He must have returned while she slept.

"Of course. Please come in," she heard him say.

She tiptoed down the flights and heard them talking in the living room.

Veyl sensed her presence and called out. "Don't listen out there, Clara. Come and join us."

Clara went in to see two men sitting in chairs opposite Veyl. One was in a policeman's uniform. "Sit down, please, Clara. These two policemen wish to ask questions. Apparently, something terrible happened after we left the party early last night. I'll let Officer Lewis explain."

The two men were fixated on Clara's body, clearly visible through the fragile nightdress. The plain clothes one, Lewis spoke.

"Two people were discovered dead, and the host's teenage daughter is missing, believed to be abducted. We have a list of all the guests. I understand that you and one other young lady accompanied Doctor Veyl to the party?"

"Yes, myself and our maid, Annie."

"The doctor tells me the three of you left early. What was the reason?"

A whisper in her mind… Veyl. He was doing that thing that Falcon had done, talking into her mind. 'You were poorly. A headache', Veyl said. 'And, Clara… distract them, be clumsy with your closed legs'.

"It was a lovely party. I wanted to stay, but a migraine came upon me. Doctor Veyl demanded he take me home. He doesn't like to see me suffer." Clara said, shuffling in the chair and opening her legs slightly.

"I see. And what is your relationship with the good doctor?"

"He's my teacher. I'm his apprentice learning his art." She told him, watching the uniformed policeman scribble in a small notebook.

"Did you notice anyone giving undue attention to any of the women or, indeed, yourself?"

She shook her head. "Everyone behaved in a polite, courteous manner."

As she spoke, her enhanced senses heard not just the graphite lead in the uniformed policeman's pencil, laying itself onto the paper, but footsteps on the stairs. She knew it could only be Ruth. Annie slept in a bed chamber on the ground floor—the one which was Maggie's.

"Would you excuse me, please. I am not in a proper form of attire to be sitting here with you males. I'll put on a dress and return."

She dashed out of the room and flew up the stairs, catching Ruth about to descend the final flight.

"Return to the bedroom," she told her, using the voice. *"Don't utter a sound."*

Ruth turned and walked slowly up the stairs, just as the two policemen came out of the room. Clara pushed Ruth around the corner at the top, as one of the men looked up the flight of stairs. It was the plainclothes one. He turned to Veyl. "Your young female apprentice is a fine-looking woman. Where did you find such a beauty?"

"Ha," Veyl said, a smile about him. "She found me. She came as a patient asking if I could cure her migraines. She seemed curious about the work I do using chemicals… well… you saw how pretty she is… and I'm a bachelor. I offered her a position."

"You're a very lucky man. I'm approaching a similar age as you, and I, too, am without a wife."

"Perhaps you would care to join us for dinner one evening. I'm sure she has friends she can select from to invite for dinner." Veyl said.

"Well. That's very kind."

"I'll be in touch," Veyl said.

"Oh, yes. Excellent. Thank you."

Veyl saw them to the door and then went to Clara's bedroom.

He marched straight in. "Well done, Clara. I'm pleased. He turned to Ruth, standing naked by her side. "And how are you? Have you learnt your lesson?"

Ruth stayed silent.

"You can speak now, if you wish," Clara said, realising she was still under the spell of the voice.

"I wish to leave. You have no right to keep me here," Ruth said.

"I'm afraid she has thoughts still of leaving," Clara said.

"I see," Veyl remarked. He rubbed his chin. *"Go to that chair, Ruth, and lean over the back of it."*

Ruth obeyed the voice.

Clara knew what was coming as she watched him unbuckle his belt. He slid it from the loops on his trousers and passed it to Clara. "Punish her."

"What? Me?"

"Yes, you. I want to see you travel further down your path of transformation. You are not a mere mortal, and you must learn to keep these weak entities in their place—obedient."

Clara knew there was no point in saying no. She reluctantly took hold of the belt and moved up to get in position behind Ruth.

"Good. Now, I want you to strip her bottom of skin with that tool I just gave you. If you fail, I'll command you over that chair, and demonstrate how to do it"

Clara shivered, lifted the belt high and swung it with all her strength. It slammed into Ruth's buttocks, causing the young woman to scream out, as a red stripe slowly grew across her cheeks. She raised the belt again."

"Stop. Wait until the sting grows worse before striking again." Veyl told her. He crouched down to look into Ruth's face. "Now, young lady. I want your oath that you'll not try to escape. Give me your word."

Ruth shook her head.

"Again," Veyl said and stayed watching Ruth's face as the belt found flesh. "Again," he said, and Clara struck again.

The oddest thing, Clara thought. She got pleasure out of the moment the belt struck. It excited her, in an unsuspected way. She felt her vaginal juices starting to flow. How can this be? She stopped, hand poised, waiting for Veyl's word. But it was all she could do not to bring it down.

"Do you promise not to try to run off?" She heard Veyl ask the sobbing girl.

"Yes, yes… Yes!"

"Fuck it," Clara thought and brought the belt down anyway, not once, but twice, before Veyl said, "Stop!"

He stood up. "Didn't you hear her. She's promised."

"So what?" Clara said and struck again. Each slap, each red line, each yelp was like another fingertip rub around her clitoris. The two were connected, and she wanted to orgasm. Fuck the fact that it was a trade—Ruth's pain: her ecstasy.

"Ah, I sense you're enjoying it. Carry on then if you wish." He said.

So she did, only ceasing when her knees buckled and she groaned in absolute bliss, dropping the belt and falling back to sit on the bed, her eyes closed while she spun in the stars. I was wondering why she was that way, when Veyl kissed her passionately on the lips and she responded.

She opened her legs and broke the kiss. "Take me. I want you to give me another orgasm."

Veyl stood up. "As lovely an invite as that is, I'm afraid I must refuse on this occasion. You've presented me with a gift," he said, and pointed at Ruth's exposed, blistering, red-hot bottom. He went up to Ruth, dropped his trousers and pants, and slammed himself into her swollen arse, banging her hard until he let out a deep groan and fell back to sit on the bed next to Clara.

After a few minutes, he stood and pulled his pants and trousers up.

Leave her there. I'll fetch some ointment to soothe and heal it within a few hours.

True to his word, he left, whilst Clara put her with Ruth's whimpering, and wondered at her own actions and the fact that she drew pleasure from hurting another so. What was she becoming?

Veyl returned and gave a small jar to Clara. Rub the cream on thickly, leave her there, and join me in the basement where the cells are. I have dinner waiting for you. Bring Annie too. She can share your feast.

Clara, with Annie, unblinking eyes, following, moved along the passage to where Veyl waited outside a cell.

There you are. "Your feast is in there. You can feed from both sides of the table; her neck is long and slender, her blood fresh and young. Clara reached the cell and peered in to see a young girl, pretty, with light blonde hair, and wearing a fine dress, barely twelve years old.

"She's but a child, Veyl. Surely not?"

"Young and tender to be sure. She wet herself when I grabbed her, but young blood is like nectar, the finest wine of all. I brought her to give you a treat for being compliant. Look, "he said, "best be quick, your Annie has already started."

Clara saw Annie at the girl's neck. The little angel was bound feet and hands and could do nought but sob and cry in terror. Clara did not want to add to it. But then, Annie lifted her head, turned, licked spillage from the sides of her mouth, and smiled.

The smell of blood met Clara's nostrils and filled her with hunger, like being addicted to sugar. How could she resist? She fought herself and lost. The girl's blood tasted like the richest wine. She drank slowly, savouring the fine tones of many metals. She looked up briefly at Annie, "***Enough, stop. I want the rest, all of it. Leave.***"

Annie left, and Clara continued until the young girl was empty. She wiped her mouth, turned to Veyl, "What with her now?"

"I'll carry her to the river and drop her in. You'd do best to go and check on your whipping post, Ruth."

Ruth

Chapter 14: Ruth

Clara walked into her bedroom. Ruth was still gripping the chair, but her bottom looked much better. ***"Leave the chair. Your penalty is paid."***

Ruth stood up, threw stab-your-heart-dagger looks at her. "Why were you so cruel to me?"

"I wasn't. I was making sure all thoughts of escaping were driven out of your pretty head because if they weren't, he would take hot branding irons to you and red-hot pokers. You should thank me for the lesser pain."

"I won't be making any attempts to escape. Who is he?"

"Put some clothes on. Find some in the wardrobe. You're the same fit as me."

As Ruth dressed, Clara said, "The doctor is a vampire."

Ruth turned. "They're just myths."

"As you wish. You'll witness for yourself soon enough."

There was a fluttering, the smell of the approaching night, she sensed him—Falcon. Clara turned to see the window partially open. "I think we're about to receive a visitor."

The window flew open. Falcon stepped through.

"Hello, Falcon. And what do we owe this visit to?"

He smiled as his wings folded into his black cloak. "I just missed not chatting with you under the Taxas Bacatta, and you left the party a bit early."

"I had to help Veyl."

"Introduce me then to your lovely bed-mate," Falcon said, as he saw Ruth over by the wardrobe.

"Ruth, come and meet a friend."

Ruth, only in underwear and carrying a dress, walked over to stand by Clara's side.

"My, two beautiful ladies and no lover in sight. I saw Veyl, heading for the Thames, a child in his arms. He seemed troubled in flight. I'd be wary when he returns. It looks to me, he's weaker and needs to feed."

Clara went to the dressing table and returned. "Here, Ruth, eat three cloves, now. He won't bite you, or if he does, he'll stop immediately."

Ruth took them in her hand and then looked up at Clara. "You jest?"

"Best do as she says," Falcon told her.

Ruth tore three cloves and chewed them with a face that made Clara and Falcon laugh.

"Let's sit and talk. I think he may go off and feed. We sense each other when close, so I'll warn you if he approaches."

"Where do you live?" Clara asked, sitting down on the side of the bed.

"Everywhere. And all over London on the rooftops." Falcon replied.

"In winter?" She asked.

"I fly south with the birds."

"Show Ruth your wings?" Clara said.

"Oh, I see. A disbeliever." Replied Falcon.

A sound like an umbrella opening, one that had not been opened for a long time, and the folds sticking, resisting opening; and then he stood, two large bat wings, one from each shoulder that spread out two to three arm's length, either side, across the room.

"Who wants to fly with me?"

Ruth stepped forward. "That's amazing," she said, and touched the wings. "I will. Take me far away."

Clara shook her head at Falcon, but she was behind, so Ruth never saw."

"Come on then. A quick flight and then I'll bring you back."

"No. Fly me home."

Falcon shook his head. "No. He'll take it out on Clara, and no matter where you go, he'll come and steal you in the night—not to be his sex toy, but to torture you over and over until he's bored with you. Better you stay until I kill him."

Falcon came up to Ruth, "Face away so I can hold you beneath me as we fly."

Ruth turned. He wrapped his arms around her and walked backwards with her to the window.

"Trust me," he said, and then toppled backwards out into the dusk.

Clara rushed to the window to see them falling as he twisted, opened his wings, flapped them, and then he soared with Ruth below him, off into the darkening sky.

He said 'kill'. Was it possible? But then, she's half transformed. That bitch who bit her, sucked her blood briefly; that was it. Something is now in her blood. Could Veyl reverse it with his potions? Could she be normal again?

A whispering in her head. 'He isn't coming back tonight. I sensed his thoughts. You're both safe until midday tomorrow'.

It was Falcon, on the wing, and circling the house high above. She knew—her senses connecting with his mind, looking through his eyes; London below, the river, the East End, the docks, the alleys and doorways where she had grown familiar with since…

…since… a party. Her mother announced a dance. A masked ball. Yes, a memory. Bloomsbury. Her home, but even if she found it, she would still need to hunt and kill. The drapes moved as she sat on the bed, lost in renewed memories.

Falcon swept in—Ruth still in his arms. He put her down on the floor. Clara looked to see her laughing and excited. "Fantastic. Thank you."

"Falcon. You said 'kill him'. Is that possible?"

He smiled. "He has to be weaker, not have fed for a while, and I must be gorged with the metal from many young people."

"Children?" She asked.

"The strongest metal. Yes."

"Isn't that so cruel?"

"Yes, it is. But when you're a vampire, you see the world for what it really is."

"I don't understand," Clara said.

Falcon came up close to her. His hand reached out for her, his wings folding in. "Make love with me in that soft four-poster bed, with Ruth beside us, and I'll give you a plan for the future and explain your past and why he took you."

Falcon kissed her. Ruth watched on, but then suddenly said, "Sleep with him. He knows how we can escape this web. He whispered to me as we flew."

Clara broke the kiss. "Are you sure he won't be back?"

"Yes. He wishes to strengthen. He'll hunt all through the night and rest on the rooftops after. It happens when you feed too much. You lose the strength to fly until the metal you took is spread throughout your body. It takes a while if you gorge."

"I'm not going to be blackmailed into sleeping with you, Falcon," Clara said. "To suggest that is just so cheap of you."

"It was only an idea. No one is forcing you." Falcon said.

"I'll sleep with you if you help us escape and kill Veyl," Ruth said.

Falcon looked at her and said, "A fine offer, but no, your price is too high. I can offer support, knowledge, and information to you if you have sex with me, and Clara lies next to us."

There was a faint click. Clara knew that sound—the mirror. She turned to see two figures emerging, Maggie and Eric.

"Ah, this is where they went to. I thought Veyl had killed them both. How clever." Falcon said.

Ruth wanted to know more. Clara told her, but all the time, she stared at Eric. His face was normal, and he was a beautiful-looking man.

They spoke with each other for several hours, with much of their conversation around the idea of killing Veyl. The most reluctant was Clara, who reminded everyone what failure would mean if they tried and the doctor still lived; the consequences were unthinkable. Maggie tended to side with her.

"I've known him the longest. He has many devices of torture. The chair he loves using is the least painful. Has he not shown you his so-called tropical greenhouse?" Maggie said.

Clara shook her head.

"Pray he never does," Maggie warned them.

"I thought vampires could only be killed by a wooden stake through the heart," Clara said.

"Pure myth, like not being able to walk in sunlight," Falcon told her. "And not casting a reflection in a mirror, or throwing a shadow—all stuff of fiction and story books."

"How, then?"

"Poison. Bad blood," Falcon said.

"What's that?" Maggie asked.

"If we all have sex together tonight, swapping partners and until morning, I'll share many secrets with you," Falcon said.

"Why? Why are you so focused on sex with us women?" Clara asked.

"Because it has been a long time since I've known such pleasure. Tell them, Maggie." Falcon said.

"Falcon was the doctor's apprentice once, but by his real name. Veyl caught us having sex together and bit Falcon, drawing much metal from his veins. Falcon made a terrible error, as he did not succumb so readily and bit Veyl's throat in a struggle. He wasn't a vampire up to that point, but afterwards... after he escaped due to the pain he caused Veyl, he realised that one act had transformed him."

Clara was looking all the time at Eric, who never took his eyes from her. Ruth kept looking at Falcon, as did Maggie, clearly remembering their pleasure together.

"So, orgy for the joy of being and enlightenment, or not?" Falcon asked.

"Yes," Maggie said.

There was a tap on the door. They all turned, most in sudden fright, thinking maybe Veyl was back, but not Falcon. He knew he wasn't. It was zombie Annie.

"I he... r...d talk..ing," she muttered almost inaudibly.

"Ah, the very instrument of poison we can use to kill Veyl," Falcon said. "Beckon her in. We'll not leave her out."

"But she's dead," Clara said. "Touch her, feel her skin."

Eric seemed to tear up as he looked at her. "Poor young lass, to be alive and dead at the same time. Falcon, can she feel anything, any joy?"

Falcon shook his head. She is in the most miserable of all states of awareness. Her insides are hung at the edge of upper decomposition, which means she rots away extremely slowly, but will still be feeling the pain of it, until her flesh drops away, and she is all but skeleton. As for feeling pleasure... I doubt it, but I know not for sure."

"I'll sleep with her," Eric said to everyone's surprise. "My heart goes out to her, and if I can throw pleasure into her ice-cold shell, then I will."

"Come here, Annie," Clara said.

"Maggie came up to her, unblinking, expressionless. A pretty zombie with a face of Titanium white. *"These are friends. You will note bite them, nor me."*

Annie just stared. There was no sign of acknowledgement. "Do you understand?"

Annie nodded.

"Good. Take off your clothes and get into bed, please."

She removed her clothes, and they all watched, witnessing her terrible, dried-up, bloodless scars. Falcon looked at Clara.

"I did not drain her, then?"

Clara shook her head.

"This is our fault and Veyl's." He said. Clara watched as Falcon went up to Annie, wrapped his arms around her and said, "You poor, dead young woman. You should never have ended up in this state." He kissed her oh, so gently on the lips, a mouth once lined with red, and pulsing life—hope; now grey, dead, and cold like touching ice.

Clara looked on. Did she see the making of a tear in his eye?

He let Annie go, and they watched her get under the covers.

"I'll try to give her joy first. A difficult task, as I'm not certain if it's possible for someone dead and living to feel ecstasy." Falcon said to the stunned others.

"Can we not end her life?" Clara asked him.

"It would mean taking her into the garden, making a large fire and setting her onto it so she cannot escape. Her sufferance would be truly terrible. Nothing short of destruction can kill someone already dead." Falcon said.

Maggie and Ruth were undressing, Clara saw, and decided to do the same. "And you, Eric, and you, Falcon."

Eric went up to Falcon. "I'll try with Zombie Annie first. My heart is still pure. Yours is not."

"True. But can you manage it? My heart is less feeling. It might make you sick, once you put it into her rotting interior."

"We'll see. I'm hopeful my soul, still intact, might give life where none exists." Eric said.

"Oh, a God believer, then. Are you?"

"I believe in love. If that is God, then yes." Eric replied and got into the bed next to Annie.

Clara, Ruth, and Maggie were left standing with Falcon. "How will you manage this, Falcon. Three women beside you. Will you have us one at a time?"

Falcon giggled. "You know little of vampires," he said, but then, midway, instead of being in front of them, he was finishing his short sentence from behind. Nobody saw him move. One moment he was there, clear for all to see, the next instant, he was behind.

They each turned, caught a glimpse of him, but then felt his touch on each of their backs, simultaneously. They turned again.

"I'll have you all at the same time. I have the speed; you three beauties have everything I need. You should get in and squeeze those two away over to the edge." He said, pointing at Maggie and Eric.

As they went to get in, something extraordinary happened. "Annie let out a loud, deep moan, and as everyone looked, they saw her body vibrating like a reed in the throat of a brass musical instrument. Eric was battling to hold onto her, as he, too, let out a deep groan of ecstasy.

Clara looked at Falcon, mind-connected, and asked by thought alone, 'Is this possible?'

'We must wait and see what happens now. She cannot live again, empty of blood'. Falcon mind-said.

Clara went over to the couple and whispered into Eric's ear as he lay there on top of zombie Annie, enjoying the peace of bliss. Eric opened his eyes and stared at her.

"Was she ever a vampire fully, or was she partially?" He asked in a whisper.

"I fed on, her and Falcon thought he'd taken the last drop, but it seems he didn't," Clara replied.

"And she died? You're certain of it?"

Clara nodded.

"From my knowledge, she is half a vampire. I can do as you ask, but it would make me one then. I don't wish to be."

"What, then?" Clara asked him.

"Falcon must save her. He should make her a full vampire. I know of no way to turn one back into a full human being."

Clara turned to Falcon. "Let her bite you, Falcon. Save her from this misery."

Falcon came over to her. "It would give her a life back, and she'd be immortal, but I don't really want her as my wife. I want you to be that."

Ruth had obviously heard. "Did someone mention immortal?" she asked.

"If Falcon drank from you and then you from him, when your teeth show, you become a full vampire but forever-bonded to him," Clara explained.

"I have a congenital illness. My life expectancy is less than thirty years. I don't wish to die so young."

Falcon smiled and said, "I want Clara as my wife, but three for the price of one is a good bargain. If Clara agrees to do the same with me as you, I'll save poor Annie, too. It will give us a way of killing Veyl, as well."

Clara looked at Annie, grey and lost. She felt the heavy burden of guilt. But...

"I'm with child, that of Eric's."

Everyone stared.

"I'm going to a father?"

Falcon looked sad. "You'll shortly miscarry, Clara. The universe does not allow issues into the world from Vampire to mortal conception. I'm sorry to tell you."

"But, I'm not a full vampire."

"No, but your blood carries the pathogen that makes you halfway. If you feed from me, the pathogen is strengthened, and you'll inherit my powers and immortality. You all will, once I have fed from you first. Your blood will mix with mine, and then when you feed from me, you receive the mixture. It bonds us forever." Falcon said.

"I've eaten garlic," Clara said.

"And I," Ruth said.

"I can still bite, but it will hurt and poison me. I only take a small amount before you feed from me. It won't kill me, but it'll make it difficult."

"I know a remedy," Eric said. "Urine neutralises the garlic. You two, Clara and Ruth, must drink liquid from my bladder.

"I can do that," Clara said.

"What will it taste like?" Ruth asked.

"Warm, salty, slightly bitter, warm water. It'll do you no harm. It is often used as a medicine for certain ailments, where uric acid and electrolytes, imbibed daily, soothe joint pains."

"Okay. I can do that too."

"Right, a plan of action then. We have only tonight. You two drink from Eric's bladder. Then Maggie lies with him, and you two and Annie will mate with me. I'll feed on you three as you each orgasm. After the bliss, you each drink from my neck, just a little. Agreed?"

They shook their heads.

"You'll need to tell Annie to bite as well, or else it won't counter your earlier command," Falcon told her.

Clara nodded. "Okay, Eric. Get that hosepipe of yours up out from between your legs and stand up. Gravity helps one wee."

Sex, Blood & Immortality

Chapter 15: Sex, Blood & Immortality

Ruth and Clara had consumed urine. The garlic was effectively neutralised. They lay with Annie between them, on their backs. Eric was having fervent sex with Maggie, shaking the bed with their lust. Falcon pulled back the covers and said, "Open your legs, and you, Ruth and Clara, each pull one of Annie's legs towards you."

They did as he asked, and Falcon looked down at them and uttered, "Three beautiful women, six breasts, and three beautiful vagina's to share bliss with. How lucky can a vampire get? I think you'll now see the benefits of becoming fully-fledged vampire brides."

The women didn't know what happened. I was as though three Falcons were in bed with them. Not once did any of them notice him move except to lunge into them; his face always above each of them, his penis only removed long enough to return at the right moment for the next thrust. They orgasmed sequentially, Ruth first, Annie second, and finally, Clara.

He waited until they were in bliss, and then he bit into each of them, drawing at least a pint of their metal, so it surged, mixed and bubbled with his own. As if sleeping gas had been sprayed into the room, they all fell asleep.

When they woke, Falcon said, "Bite me. I've bitten you and drawn metal from you. Feed on me until I tell you to stop. Immortality waits— no death, a life when you can walk in the day as well as the night, and once we're rid of Veyl, a life of wealth, class and wonder."

*"Annie, you can bite now, but just Fal*con," she said, pointing at him. *"No one else, unless I say."*

And she did. She took to Falcon's throat, as a child has a first encounter with ice cream, as he lifted his chin and smiled. Clara watched the grey deadness in her naked body begin to glow pale pink. Life—Falcon's metal, her metal, coursing in her veins, the impossible happening before her eyes.

She looked at Ruth and saw she was spellbound watching dead Annie, there, sucking at Falcon, her hero. Before Clara could say anything to deter her, she sprang forward and was at the other side of his neck.

"Annie, stop." She said with the voice.

Annie looked up at her, blood dripping from the corners of her mouth. "But it tastes so good."

"Yes, Annie. But enough now. You need to pretend to be a zombie. Do you understand that? *Whenever Veyl is here, be zombie.*"

Annie nodded.

"Ruth, I think that's enough," Clara said. But Ruth didn't stop. Clara looked at Maggie and Eric. They were both watching Ruth, too.

"Eric, Maggie, drag her off, quickly. She's taking too much." Clara called out.

There was no need. Falcon took his hands up to Ruth, pushing her off. *"Enough. No more."*

He used the voice on her, Clara realised. He had that too.

"Clara. You know. I've lost a lot of metal. When you feed on me, the taste and richness will make you greedy. You must take from me and stop taking without me pushing you away." Falcon said. "Taste me and let go. Master your transformation. Control is everything."

Clara could already smell the iron, the copper, and silver in his blood. Her fang teeth were extending, her mouth was salivating, his soft throat was just there in front of her, ready for her to transform forevermore into an immortal. Had the sex, the smell of blood, the company of the others not muddied her thoughts, she might not have done it; she did—sinking her teeth into him, and sucking his gorgeous metal, which tasted of the very finest wine.

She drank greedily, only just recalling his words that he must stop on her own accord. She fought her desire to continue and pulled away, breathless. Her body buzzed, and she felt more alive than she had ever known; her thoughts were quicker, her heart stronger, her feelings more powerful, and her senses lifted to another degree.

Falcon groaned and slowly lifted his head from the pillow. "A little bit too much, but at least you broke the feeding under your own control. Well done. Now, would you like a maiden flight with me?"

"But I have no wings."

"Imagine in your mind that you do." He told her.

She closed her eyes and thought of herself with bat wings, and something never felt or heard before happened: her shoulder blades seemed to move, and she heard a sound like thin silk being ripped apart. She felt them then, as nerves, fresh muscles, sinews, and small, slender bones connected with her torso. It felt like she had another pair of arms, and then that exciting noise of a sticky umbrella opening. She opened her eyes, felt a wing on either side, wiggled them and laughed out loud.

She stood up and twirled, shouting out to the others, "Look, look, I have wings."

One of the wings slapped into Ruth's face as she twirled.

"Watch out," Ruth cried out. "That stung."

"When you fly, start with a glide. To go higher, bend back from your waist and flap. When you land, tilt your wings back, which stalls them just as you are about to touch down." Falcon told her.

"Okay," Clara replied.

"Good, come with me to the window."

She soared up over the yew tree, after diving down, thinking for a moment she'd smash into the ground before remembering Falcon's guidance. It saved her. This was so exciting, she thought, circling the tree, and sweeping under Falcon coming around it from the other way.

"Clara. We need to return. He's on his way back." She heard him shout as he swept past.

"What?"

"Go back to the bedroom. Get everyone to pretend nothing has changed," he shouted, and then flew away.

As she returned to the window, she realised both Ruth and Annie were going to be a big problem. Ruth isn't going to tolerate him fucking her, and Annie is not going to play a zombie maid.

As she climbed in through the window, an idea came to her.

"And how was your maiden flight?" Maggie asked.

"Maggie, Eric, everyone, Veyl's on his way. You two need to hide behind the mirror. *Ruth, you are not a vampire, and you'll do his bidding. Annie, your mind is slow. You're dead and a zombie.*"

Would the voice still work?

She looked at Ruth, who seemed to just relax back and fall asleep on the bed. Annie put on her maid's uniform and walked out of the bedroom. Clara watched Maggie give a wave and close the mirror. Clara put her wings tightly away and checked her back and her neck in the mirror. The bite marks were gone, and there was no sign of having wings. She sprayed the room with perfume and pissed on the floor by the chair Ruth had been bent over, then she got into bed and hugged her whilst pretending to be asleep.

Twenty minutes later, she heard the distant sound of the street door opening and closing, his footsteps on the wooden boards—her senses were so enhanced, she heard Annie, apron rustling as she stepped out into the hall, and curtsied. "G.. Get y...o..u somet..hing?" Clara heard her say.

"No, thank you, Annie. My, I do declare there's a little colour in your cheeks. I expect that's Clara's work with face powder and makeup. A good improvement."

She heard his footsteps on the stairs, the air stirring as he walked down the hallway towards her door. The hairs on her neck stood up, warning her of the approach of a dangerous animal, and that is certainly what he was.

He entered the room, walked over to the bed, pulled back the covers, and stared at them both, lying naked and hugging each other.

He shook both awake and said, "While I undress, you, Ruth, turn onto your stomach. When she is lying flat, you, Clara, lie on top of her with your legs wide apart. I'll fuck her beneath you and pretend I'm fucking you."

He started to undress. Clara whispered into Ruth's mind. 'Take it, don't rebel, wait for my word and then bite the fucker and draw his metal from him, as I do the same. Not before I say. I know exactly the moment to strike'.

Veyl was naked. Clara did as she was told and was lying on top of the upturned Ruth. Veyl gently lay himself down on top of Clara, smiled, and said, "Her arse is lovely and tight. Before me, no one had ever entered it."

He grunted and kissed Clara lightly on her lips as he forced his hard penis into Ruth's rectum, straining against the organic resistance, and in rebellion against the intrusion of an object it had never been designed to accept. Rush squealed in discomfort and pain.

"Hmm," Veyl said, "I believe it's got even tighter since I was in this lovely warm slippery place, earlier. Excuse my sudden forceful movement, please, Clara."

Clara felt him pull back slightly, and then lunged forward with such great force that she heard the muted sound of soft tissue tearing, and Ruth letting out a sharp gasp of shock and pain.

"There," Veyl whispered, "All the way in. I'll start slowly and look at your beautiful face."

Clara reached up her hands to the back of his head. "Kiss me with passion," She whispered to him. "Keep kissing me, slide up and down against my breasts as you enjoy her bottom. When your heart is beating fast and your blood is pumping with lust, take it out of her and put it in me. Finish in me."

He broke the kiss, kept moving, stared at her. "I'm surprised. You wish me to fuck your vagina?"

"No. I want you to fuck me in my vagina. You're to look into my eyes all the time. I want to see the fire of lust in them, and the explosion into orgasm. It's what you most want. Is it not?"

"Yes. Do you wish to transform? If so, I need to bite you and then you bite me."

"Oh, doctor. Let me think on it after I've shared an orgasm with you." She said. He moved faster, thrusting in and out of Ruth, before removing his penis and sliding it into Clara.

"Oh, that's so fulfilling," she whispered, like a spider luring him into her trap. She sensed Falcon was close and mind-spoke to him, 'Falcon, Ruth, and I are going to attempt to drink Veyl, dry. When I say now, come and help'.

"Faster, love… faster. Let yourself go." She said loudly. "Use your gift of speed, in-out, Ruth, in-out, me." She spurred him on, wanting him to lose all his thoughts and clever wit. "Come inside my arse," she whispered to him— "my gift to you on this, our first copulation."

He could not believe such an invitation, "Lift your legs back, then, so I can make a ball of you, and make it easier to pound you there."

"Best if you let me lift first and bid Rush to move to one side."

He nodded. She lifted, and he removed himself from Clara.

"Ruth, move to one side, please. Spare yourself. I want him all to myself."

She felt Ruth shift, dropped herself down, and rolled back so her knees went down on the pillow on each side of her head.

"Perfect, Clara. Absolutely, bloody, perfect." Veyl told her and plunged his cock in.

She had never been penetrated in such a taboo place. She had heard from the whores laughing and telling, outside the ale houses in the east end of such, and that men loved it there best. It felt very uncomfortable, even painful, when he was all the way in, and with such a large member, it felt like his bloody arm was up there to the elbow.

He pushed against her ankles, holding them locked onto the pillows as he rose and careered down, like a thick spear, falling from the keep of a castle to embed itself in her soft interior.

"Yes, yes, faster, faster, I'm nearly there." She cried out, as she mind-told Ruth and Falcon, 'Be ready, you two'. Then she mind told Annie to come up the stairs and wait, quietly, outside the bedroom door. Falcon mind-whispered back, 'I'm outside the window. He'll sense me this close if you don't intoxicate him fully with your sexual sacrifice, Clara'.

'Oh, no need to worry about that, he's fully in, and he'll pay for this terrible sacrifice, the fucking bastard'. She mind-replied.

Veyl removed his penis and instead pushed it into her vagina. He thrust several times, groaning and shaking.

"I've just come, but I can come again, a more powerful one if you'll do me a favour of passion?" Veyl suddenly said, "Open your mouth, now, Clara, I beg you."

No sooner did she obey then she was gagging, and desperately trying to hold back the vomit coming up her throat, but there was no need—his cock was stuck down it, and his hand around her throat, squeezing it tightly to his cock, as his seed pumped out and merged with her bile.

He pulled it out and fell to one side as she unfolded her legs and whispered, "I came as you shot your seed into my soul."

He sighed and closed his eyes, floating in his damned bliss.

'*Now!*' she mind-said to the others, and took his throat in her extended teeth.

"What?" he cried out, but was cut short as Ruth bit deeply into the other side, into his artery, and sucked like a leech. The drapes flew back. Falcon swept in, threw back the covers, leapt onto the bed, and bit into Veyl's femur inside his thigh. The door flew open, and Annie lumbered in and joined them on the bed, finding Veyl's other thigh held a similar artery to feed upon.

Veyl did not provide a meal so readily. He fought with the full strength of the legendary Hercules, kicking them off, one at a time, punching, kicking, as each seized a part of him in their mouths again. It was only the mirror opening, and Eric, along with Maggie, who saved the day—stepping out, dashing forward and holding Veyl down, gripping him with revenge and hatred, as the others sucked and sucked the metal from him, turning him white, and then grey.

Only when he lay still and no longer breathing—did they let up, and wiping their mouths, looked at each other.

It was several minutes before anyone spoke.

"Is he really dead?" Maggie asked the vital question that no one else wished to ask.

"Falcon? Is he dead?" Clara asked.

He shook his head. "No. I told you. It is hard to kill a vampire. You have to destroy him completely. If his shell is left and anything living bites him, he'll activate again."

"Fire, then. We'll hang him in the yew tree and set fire to it. Will that work?" Clara asked.

Falcon nodded. "I hope so, but he's been around for a very long time. I was just his apprentice, but it seems to me that his bones will still be here. We need to destroy those, too. The heat of the tree is not enough. We'll need to take his skeleton, and in some way—I know not how—crush it to dust and scatter it so as not one tiny particle can start to combine with another."

"If we don't," asked Maggie. "How long before he rises again?"

Falcon shrugged. "I've no idea."

"We burn him now, then. We'll rest and find a way to crush him out of existence afterwards." Clara offered.

"Okay. Let's do it. We can fly up and carry him into the branches of the yew," Falcon said.

"I'll fetch alcohol from his laboratory," Maggie said.

"I'll find matches and I insist that you light the fire," Ruth said.

"It seems we have a plan. We need a fallback. God forbid if we fail to destroy the monster, Veyl." Eric said.

"Fallback?" Ruth asked.

Clara answered, "She means, what's our plan if he somehow survives?"

"Let's think about it after we've burnt him," Ruth said.

"You do realise," Maggie said, with a kind of sadness across her face, that you are now all vampires just like him.

"No." Falcon rebuked. Vampires yes. Immortal, up to a point, but nothing like that evil bastard." He pointed at the naked, grey corpse on the four-poster bed.

"Come on, Falcon, we'll fly him to the tree," Clara said.

The others watched as they did.

River Monster

Chapter 16: River Monster

The fire and the death of the yew tree was like a ceremony of life and death, with no hope of renewal, Clara thought, as she watched the soaring flames begin to lick at the body of Veyl, lying there, due to her and Falcon's hands, in the upmost branches of the tree, where the heat would be most intense. How long had that beautiful tree stretched its multiple arms out to find the light, and how many people had sheltered beneath it?

Ruth began clapping as Veyl ignited. "Oh, look, he's burning up like a firework. Such joy!"

Clara had to admit, she felt joy, too, but she was more concerned about how to ensure he stayed dead. She turned to Falcon, "What will we do to destroy his skeleton?"

Maggie heard. "I know men who steal from graves. They'll bury it or sell it on for cutting up."

Falcon shook his head. "That won't work. I have a better idea."

"Really? What?"

"One of you three needs to have sex with a miller, without killing him. We'll use his millstone to grind his bones to dust and mix it in with his flour."

"Annie's pretty and doesn't talk much, and she won't be very useful with the work itself," Clara said.

"No. I'll do it. Anything to end the bugger's existence." Ruth said.

The following day, they were up bright and early. It needed Falcon and Clara to fly up and throw the skeleton down, which shattered. Ruth, Eric, and Maggie collected the bones and put them in a sack. Annie watched on, smiling but not helping.

"How do we get Veyl's driver to take us?" Clara asked.

"Veyl has a small fortune in his vault," Maggie said. "I saw him once, opening it. I know the combination. He has a copper tube to the driver's house, like on the ships' speaking tubes. He paid him well, but let him take girls, for sex—you understand, often giving them afterwards for Veyl to feed on. Come on, I'll show you."

They all followed her, except Annie, which Clara realised was a huge mistake afterwards.

They were in the lab. Maggie carefully removed all the phials, bottles and jars from one of the bookcases. She pulled it, and it swung open. A room of stone and steel was revealed. Maggie turned, smiled and said, "He boasted to me once, said he could use tunnels in here to travel underground all over London. The house was built in an age of struggle: The English Civil War."

She pointed left, "Metal vault," pointed right, "speaking tube."

She walked to the far side.

Clara watched as she pushed a brick, and the entire wall slid away to reveal a set of tunnels with signs above them. She left them, went to the vault, turned several numbered wheels, and pulled the metal door open.

Falcon, Eric, Clara and Ruth walked over to join her and looked inside.

"So much coin, gold, silver and jewels," Eric said.

"It appears that not only are we immortal, but rich beyond our wildest dreams," Clara said. "Ruth, go and put on something sexy. Falcon, forget the driver, get a wheelbarrow. I've heard of a miller in Mitcham. We'll use the tunnels to get there."

Falcon shook his head. "Mitcham is south of London, a place of gypsies. I've fed on some there. It's too far to walk. I'll use the tube and call the driver. Get some notes and coins ready to give him and the miller."

The coach pulled up, and all but Annie went to it, as Maggie closed the door to the house. Falcon held the sack. The driver climbed down, and Maggie spoke to him on her own. He nodded, and she gave him the money.

Clara noted that he looked more than pleased, especially when she pointed at Ruth, who smiled at him. It was obvious that Ruth had been offered as well. She listened to the final exchange with her enhanced hearing.

"Veyl has gone abroad. Better hunting, she said. We're in charge while he's away. We'll make sure you are rewarded. Do you think young Ruth is pretty?"

"I do."

"Good. You can fuck her in the coach on our way back." Maggie said.

Clara went to Ruth, "You're part of the bargain. Are you up for fucking him to keep him sweet?"

"Sure, but I think then, you should fuck the miller. You're smarter than I am, and you'll keep him distracted better than I."

"Okay. Deal. Where's Annie?"

"I haven't seen her," Ruth said.

"Oh dear. We've made a bad error. Her mind is slow. She may have flown off to feed…"

As Clara tried to finish her sentence, there was a fluttering of wings. Clara turned to see Annie behind her, wings still out.

"Annie. Put the wings away and get in the coach." Clara said, using the voice.

Annie obeyed and stepped in and sat on the velvet.

"Her," Clara heard the driver say to Maggie, now. That's the deal."

Maggie returned to the group.

"I know, Maggie. Get the others to sit on the steps with you, while I arrange things." Clara said.

As the others went to the steps, Clara went to the coach and opened the door. *"Fuck him good, but don't feed on him,"* she told Annie.

"No need you to use the voice on me. I know my mind not good, but I am learning. Okay?"

Clara was stunned. Her mind was growing stronger. She nodded.

"Yes, pull your dress up, lie down and stay compliant. We need the stupid, rough man, to help us."

She stepped outside and said to the driver, "Don't hurt her, or I'll hurt you."

He tipped his hat, smiled a toothless grin, opened the door, and went in, as Clara went to sit with the others.

They sat together, the party that had killed Veyl, and watched as the coach rocked violently. No one felt pity for Annie. The only thing on their minds and the focus was—get rid of Veyl and live a life together in this great house full of riches.

The coach stopped rocking. The driver stepped out and climbed up to take the reins. Clara ran to the coach, opened the door, and leapt in to see Annie pushing her dress back down. "Are you okay?"

"Yes. He's different."

"How?"

He has two members. He push the two into both my holes."

Clara was intrigued. "What's his name?"

"He say, he, Claude."

Clara stepped out of the coach. "Claude. Come down here and get inside."

He stepped down, bemused. "I thought you wanted me to take you to Mitcham," he said in a coarse voice. "It's a long way."

"Yes, yes. Get inside, please."

He shrugged and stepped up into the coach. Clara followed and slammed the door shut. "Show me," she demanded.

"Show you what?"

"She says you have two."

"Do I now. Two horses?" he replied, deliberately confusing the issue, Clara thought.

"No, cocks. Show me."

"Those who get to use are allowed to see. No one else." Claude said, with insolence.

"Are you refusing to show me?" Clara pushed.

"No. As I already said, only those who get to use them can see them first."

He wanted to fuck her, too? Is it possible he could do that so quickly after having Annie? "Okay. Show me now. If you really have two, you can come to the house tonight and fuck me. In fact, you can fuck us all, except Maggie."

"All, or no deal." He told her. He'd recognised an opportunity here, she realised.

"Okay. I'll ask Maggie too, but in the end, it'll be up to her. Okay? Now, Claude, let me see."

He stood up, dropped his trousers and pants, and said, "Here. The doctor gave me a potion as a reward. I can receive a full orgasm from each, and they are greatly enhanced. If you touch them, you'll see them at full mast, so to speak."

He had two long, flaccid cocks hanging down. She had to see how they worked and reached out and touched them both. Immediately, one became fully erect, and at a size and girth she'd never encountered before. The other one was strange. It slowly became erect but arched like a huge. thick banana. She wondered about it and realised it was so it could slip underneath and enter from the rear. The two cocks seemed to expand and grow unbelievably, until they were so puffed up with blood, she could see each one tremor to the pulse of his heart.

"Is there a passage from your home to the house?" she asked him.

He nodded.

"I'll leave the doors open from the passage to our bedroom. Come at midnight. Our bedroom is on the second floor, up two flights of stairs. The bedroom door will be open. and no lights will be on. We'll all be in the four-poster bed. Bathe thoroughly before you come. Are you able to have all of us?"

"Sure. More than once each."

"Okay, now drive us, please, to Mitcham."

The coach arrived in Mitcham and stopped. The driver called down, wanting directions.

"Falcon said, I'll go up and direct him to the mill." He opened the door and climbed up. The coach started moving again. Clara took the opportunity to tell them then.

"We are to let the coach driver have all of us in our bed tonight at midnight, including you, Maggie."

"What? No…"

"He wouldn't help us unless we did. Sorry. But I promised for you. He has two penises, so you might find it interesting."

"Two?" Ruth asked.

Clara nodded. "He showed them to me and used them both on Annie here."

"He very big. You see tonight," Annie said.

"Maggie. Do you take note that I'm not asking you to sleep with the miller? I'll do that for all of us." Clara said.

"Yes. It's okay. I'll do my bit, too. Have no worries."

Clara kissed her on the cheek. Thank you."

The miller took little persuasion. He took one look at Clara, her beautiful face, fine clothes, the signs about her presence and bearing that told of nobility. Money too? And for what, so these people from a fine, rich household in London could grind their own home-grown wheat into flour for their home-baked loaves?

"Of course, our party needs a quick lesson from you on how to use the millstone, and spread the grain onto it, to mill it to the finest flour. We have but a single sack of wheat, grown in our very own estate." Clara told him.

He showed them, but on seeing the party, he had eyes staring constantly at Ruth. He went up to speak to Clara and pointed at her. "One hour with her out at the back and the money."

"No, no. You can have her and the money if we can mix our fine flour with yours. We understand your flour goes to Baker Street, London. It feeds the poor, and it's not of good quality. We are a Quaker family. Wealthy, yes. And this is why our fine wheat must benefit them."

He started to think, Clara saw.

"Ruth, the miller wishes to be introduced to you," she called out.

The miller stopped thinking as Ruth drifted over. "Yes, sir. Forgive me for being forward, but I noticed you're strong. Most men I meet are quite weedy. May I feel your sinews?"

He smiled. "Yes, of course."

"Ruth. Perhaps you might like to explore our helpful miller…" Clara said, turning to him, "…where did you say?"

"Out back," he replied.

Ruth took his hand. "But of course. Let's take our time, shall we?"

And off they went.

"Okay. Time to grind the bugger's bones." Clara told the others. They used the gears and the power of the river Wandle to raise the grinding stone, and throw the sack of bones onto the base stone. Then they lowered the millstone and engaged the gears to the waterwheel outside.

They clapped as they heard the crack and crackle of the bones being ground to dust.

"Make sure no powder or dust spurts out from the wheel," Falcon told them. "Spread around the stone. Keep watch out."

They did.

In under half an hour, they raised the stone to see. The base stone was covered with fine white grains.

"Fetch the miller's product bags, lots of them, and empty them onto the stone. We'll grind it one more time and mix it a-plenty." Falcon said.

They were on their way back to London. Together, they had diluted Veyl's powdered bones with many pounds of the miller's flour, re-bagged it into his little printed white bags, all ready to travel to Baker Street and into the loaves baked there.

Ruth told them how disappointing the miller was, barely raising any sign of excitement in her, what with him reaching orgasm on the first few thrusts, she had told them.

"Well, best then, you save that for tonight. We still have a price to pay for our driver's help and silence," Clara told her.

"Actually," Ruth replied. "I'm quite looking forward to it, since he's a bit unusual."

"Well, I'm not," Maggie said.

"Annie. How about you?" Clara asked her.

She shrugged. "I don't care. Am I allowed to feed on him?"

Clara shook her head. "No, Annie. Just be a zombie for him. If you're hungry, we'll sort it out tomorrow."

"What are we men supposed to do?" Eric asked. "When we're sleeping together and he climbs into our bed?"

Clara looked at Falcon, who stepped in to help. "We'll watch over them. Claude is a rough man. We'll ensure the women stay safe."

Midnight.

They were all together across the four-poster. Falcon and Eric were on the outside. Maggie was beside Eric, Falcon beside Clara. Between those two women were Ruth and Annie. It was dark. No oil lamp was lit.

"I'm so excited," Ruth said. "Are you sure he'll come, Clara?"

"Definitely. Like most men, his weakness is his desire to have sex with beautiful women."

"He tell me he like tight holes," Annie told them.

"Ssshh, I heard something."

They listened with their enhanced hearing. Clara was the first to say, "Footsteps, but more than one person, coming up the basement stairs near the laboratory."

"Oh, praise God, it's not." They heard Maggie say. "Did you open all the doors to the tunnels, including the one marked river?"

"Yes. Why?"

"Don't say a word. Don't resist it or you'll receive a painful sting." Maggie said in a hushed and rushed whisper.

"What is it, Maggie? What the hell is coming up those stairs?"

"His pet. A thing he found on the muddy bank of the river one day, coaxed back to life and altered by his potions. I warn you all. Let it do whatever it wants to do.

They heard it more distinctly then, a wet slithering up the stairs to the final hallway.

"Falcon, take Eric, and fly outside down to the garden with him. I'll call you back when it's safe." Clara said.

"I…" Falcon started to say.

"Listen to her, for Christ's sake. You men won't be safe." Maggie urged.

Falcon went to the window. "Come on, Eric."

No sooner had Falcon flown off with Eric then they all heard something unmentionable slide in from the hallway. Clara wished she'd lit the oil lamp. Not seeing, not knowing, made the fear so much worse. She heard it sliding, and it was towards her side of the bed. Her dead, alive again, heart sped up, as she felt it slither up onto the bed and under the covers.

A pushing between her legs—wet, slimy, and a smell of rotting, stinking fish was filling the air.

"Something wet is pushing up between my legs," Rush rasped out in a whisper."

"And mine," Annie said.

"Open your legs or it'll sting your thighs to enter you," Maggie said. "It's like an octopus, but mutated, with multiple penises at the end of its tentacles. Move with it. Give it joy and it won't hurt you."

"This is more exciting than the prospect of Claude," Ruth whispered. Which made Clara wonder what happened to him.

There was no thinking. She took Maggie's advice and opened her legs, just in time, as a thick, goo-covered thing pushed and wriggled up high inside her. Just as she got kind of used to that intrusion, another tentacle, because that was what Maggie had explained, pushed its way into her rectum. She felt each tentacle flick against the tight, stretched membrane of her anal entrance, as it slowly pushed more of its thick extensions into her.

"It's in my arse and my cunt," Annie whispered.

"Annie. Do as Maggie said, or it'll hurt you." Clara whispered to her. "It's doing the same to all of us."

There was a gagging noise, and Clara thought it was Ruth. "Are you okay, Ruth?" She whispered. The only reply she got was the sound of tortured attempts to speak through stifled vomiting.

The tentacles inside her, Clara, were like liquid bliss. They moved with care and precision, not rushed like men do, she thought. She moved with them, loving the sensation, excited by the expectation of orgasm with a monster from the deep. Two monsters: the thing and her.

Annie cried out a loud groan in the dark. Orgasm, Clara realised, and her own now on the trigger point: she let out a deep moan, as her body flooded with a release from her dead life, and for a while, she swam in the stars and the light of true death.

Time Travel

Chapter 17: Time Travel

In Baker Street, ovens were lit, and loaves were put in. They would be baked all through the night, and sent, fresh and still warm, to be distributed early in the morning, east and west, with no preference of whose mouths they'll feed—rich or poor.

The thing from the river slid away. As Clara recovered from her time in the bliss, she heard it slithering back to whence it came. She got out of bed and lit the lamp as Falcon came back in the window with Eric.

"Are you all okay?" He asked.

"I'm not sure. Maggie, Annie?" Clara told him.

"I, okay. Good sex. Gentle." Annie declared.

"I had it before. Veyl set it upon me once as a little bit of entertainment for him. I resisted. It stung me so much, I writhed in agony, and it entered me then, using my body motion to aid its sex. Better not to resist, so, yes. I'm okay." Maggie said.

"Ruth?" Clara asked.

Ruth was a greyish shade of pale—she shook her head, briefly, and said, "It put one of its tentacles down my throat. I can feel something still th…"

She could say nothing more. Everyone was mesmerised as she sat up, staring with eyes that told not of the outside world around her, but of the one within; with her mouth wide open, and her body shaking. Something started slipping out of her mouth—saliva and goo, mixed, and fell onto the counterpane.

They all backed away, leaving Ruth to the call of nature as she started gagging and choking. The tip of a tentacle became a long, squirming thing that slid out of her mouth and dropped onto the bed. Before anyone could move, it fell off and slid out of the room.

Clara watched the last of it disappear and then threw herself at Ruth, put her arms around her, and hugged her.

"The creature gave birth," Maggie said.

It was morning in London, and servants of the wealthy went to buy loaves for the household kitchens. In the east end, loaves were stolen and resold. As it went stale, the bits that were left, well… they found comfort in the stomachs of pigeons that flew and crapped. Rains came with the winter, washing their filth into the drains so it could join the human waste already running in underground pipes under the city.

In the house that was once Veyl's, a family of immortals prospered. They secured the tunnels and established roles, one of which was looking after Annie. It was decided that she must never fly off to feed on prey alone. Falcon, Ruth, or Clara would always go with her. Trying to minimise the fact that the four of them needed to take human blood, they would aim mostly to finish off the old, the mad, or those sentenced to be hanged, and reward their moral intentions by feeding to the last drop, babies born with congenital health issues—already sentenced to death by being born wrong.

Months passed. The driver, Claude, was allowed to come once a month and fuck one of them in return for his silence and servitude, and the money they paid him.

None of them had any thought that below London, the sewers were often partially blocked by fat, soap and human hair, and at one bend beneath Southwark, debris formed, and the rats watched as something began to take shape, never witnessed before. Over the months into December, a body of sorts seemed to appear in the slime and shit. It took shape, lay there, comfortable to remain trapped and waiting as other tiny molecules in the muck, continued to stick to the mass as if it knew they belonged there.

"It's sunny outside," Ruth said, standing at the bedroom window. "We should go out somewhere nice."

Clara propped herself up on the pillows, looking to see which of the others were still in bed with her. They were all there, except Ruth.

"Yes. A good idea, but come back to bed for a while and give me a cuddle. I love it when we're all together and it's chilly with no fire lit."

Ruth smiled as she walked over to the bed and got in. They snuggled up together. After a few minutes, Ruth said, "I've never had sex with a woman. What's it like?"

"Would you like to find out?" Clara asked, her eyes twinkling and playful.

"What you mean…"

Clara touched her lips with her forefinger. "Ssshh, not so loud. You'll wake the others." And kissed Ruth gently on her lips. Her hand slipped up between Ruth's legs and under her short nightdress. Ruth broke the kiss and stared into Clara's eyes. "Yes, okay."

No sooner than the words had left her mouth, Clara slid out of sight and under the covers. But her presence was still there between Ruth's opening legs, and where Clara's tongue began licking her. Ruth liked it and put her hands underneath to press Clara's head more firmly against her.

It had the effect of Clara working more urgently with her tongue, licking and flicking so rapidly that it brought young Ruth quickly to orgasm. She let out a long sighing sound, like the last dying breath of an old man or woman, weeing a little with the strength of the convulsion rippling through her body. She floated in bliss and felt Clara slide up out from under, her lips falling upon hers, and her tongue probing the inside of Ruth's.

"That was beautiful. Thank you. Better than with a man, I think."

"It's best with a man and a woman at the same time," Clara said. "I'll ask Falcon or Eric to do it on you with me, one evening."

"Okay. I'm always for discovering new experiences."

"Where did you want to go today?" Clara asked.

Ruth shrugged. "It's sunny and cold, but I think it will snow soon, probably in time for a white Christmas. What about Hyde Park, just a walk through there. We can get Claude to take us in the coach."

"Okay. We'll wait for the others to wake up naturally, have breakfast together, and then go."

Deep below London's streets, a reeking pile of human waste slowly built a shape until a skeleton was witnessed by the black rats, who immediately saw the opportunity to gnaw at the bones for the marrow inside. But as they approached, fear repelled them. It was as the clever rodents realised, the flesh hanging from those bones wasn't rotting and falling: it was growing and reddening.

Hyde Park was not as pretty as in the summer, but the open space after the claustrophobic darkness of their individual journeys that brought them all together was, Clara thought, like fresh baby's blood to a vampire, or in her former life, fresh air to a mortal.

"I used to come here with Mama and Papa," Ruth said, out of the blue as they walked along.

"Don't you wish to return to them and your family home?" Clara asked.

Ruth was quiet for a while before replying. "I'm changed. My world has changed. No. I love the family I belong to now."

"I would love to return to my life," Maggie said.

"Why don't you?" Ruth asked. "You're not changed."

Maggie smiled. "I no longer know where I came from, and because of Veyl giving me a potion that destroyed my memory, I never will."

"Falcon," Clara turned and asked him, "What about your past?"

"Ha. I was raised by a wealthy family, too. Adopted. I long ago forgot that life, but they educated me well. I'm thankful for that." He said.

"How about you, Eric? Do you not wish to return to your previous life?" Ruth asked instead of Clara. "Like Maggie, you are still mortal."

"I love Maggie. The future is that. The past..." he said, revealing no more.

Clara saw Maggie clutch his hand tighter. She'd not realised the affection between them, and was pleased they were unchanged. They were good people, unlike her, now, and the others. Yes, she thought, there was goodness still in us, but the lust in our veins made us human parasites. The reward for immortality was a denial of a heaven or a hell, or simply—the abyss, and an eternal life in the flesh. An infinite life of pleasure or pain, a future unknown. She felt sadness in her heart. There was no celebration in her soul, but gratitude that she was now out of Veyl's clutches.

They walked past normal people, some young, which made Clara see them in the passage of time: old, struggling to walk, or breathe, or in pain month after month as consumption took them or a common cold. The list of illnesses which culled the old was endless. But her, Ruth, Annie, and Falcon were immune to such malaises."

No one bothered to ask poor Annie about her wishes or her past. But she was improving. "I not want to return. We live in nice big house, sleep together in nice warm bed. It better than slum, cockroach houses, and a piece of bread a day."

Clara kissed her. "Well done, Annie. And we'll all treat you as our little sister. We'll keep you safe."

"I know. I not bright yet. I learn." She said.

Not far from them, beneath the east end, a naked figure climbed a ladder up to a metal manhole cover, lifted it, and climbed out in a dark alley. Shrewd and knowing, he stayed in the shadows waiting for the first male to slip in for a quick pee. He was patient. Had he not spent months in the dark? What were a few hours in an infinite lifespan? It was early evening when a hapless man slipped into the alley, and slipped out of life just as discreetly; Veyl sucked the life out of him, and took his clothes.

They finished dinner together. But, except for Maggie and Eric, it never quite took away their hunger.

Clara rested back in her chair and said, "I'm still hungry."

Falcon looked at her and understood. He bent over to put his mouth close to her ear. "No need for everyone to go out into the night. I know a place where we can feed and bring back prey for Annie and Ruth."

"Babies?"

"No," Falcon said. "Children in the care of a nunnery. There are several men of the cloth who regularly abuse them. Evil men. We feed on the men and bring two of the children back for the others."

"No. The children have suffered enough. We can glut on the bastard priests and take more than our fill. Annie and Ruth can take the access from us." Clara told him.

He thought about it. While he was thinking, Ruth said, "What are you two whispering about?"

Clara told her the truth.

"You always want to do good, Clara. I don't mind drinking from you, but to be honest, it's a bit like eating regurgitated food instead of fresh."

"Okay," Clara said. "You go with Falcon, then, and I'll take your access later."

Ruth stared at her. "If I agree, where will you take your fill from?"

"Not where, when. I'll take my fill from the place I gave you bliss in our bed, when you return and we all sleep together."

Ruth laughed. "You go then. I'll return the joy you gave to me this morning, and take my fill at the same time when you swim in the stars."

"Good. I'll instruct Annie…"

"You say my name." Annie interrupted. "Tell me."

Clara tried to explain.

"Stop. Too complicated. I trust you, sister. You tell me simply." Annie said.

"I'm going out with Falcon. I'll tell you when I return. Okay?"

Annie nodded.

The nunnery, in true catholic tradition, had a lodging house and a tiny school. Clara knew the children therein were being taught nothing of worldly value. They were there to serve the church as unpaid, cheap workers—and to be further put to distress by those men who, in their cloth of respectability, came to use them for sexual gratification.

Falcon and Clara landed on the rooftops. He whispered to her. "I'm used to crawling down walls using just my fingertips to find cracks to grip to. I'll go down and force open a window. Wait here."

True to his word, he slipped over the side and was back inside a minute.

"Okay. It's just below. Fly off, swing round and go through. I'll be right behind you." He told her.

She got in. Falcon whispered, "Follow me."

"Where're we going?" She whispered back.

"To see Father Clark. His bedroom is at the end of this hallway."

The hallway was lit by a dim gaslight. Clara's senses felt something, the footsteps of young ghosts, the footsteps of little boys and girls that had been taken down here in the near dark, their little hand in the safe guiding hand of a nun as it was delivered to receive the blessing of Father Clark at the end of the hall. She could hear their muted ghost screams and their whimpering as they were duly raped, over and over again, and then strangled.

She had no need to ask Falcon why they were here: the ghost children had already told her.

She was beside Falcon as he turned the handle of the door and walked in. There was a priest at a writing desk, scribbling away by lamplight.

"Good evening, Father Clark," Falcon said. "No little visitors tonight."

Clara smiled a death smile deep inside her soul, as she saw the priest believe for a moment that a ghost had just spoken to him.

"Don't you wish to turn and lay eyes on one of your wee lads?" Falcon said.

The priest turned. His face turned white as he saw Falcon.

"Why? Little Tom Smith. All grown up. And why are you here at night?" The priest said. "And how in heaven's name did you gain entrance?"

"It doesn't matter. I brought my pretty girlfriend to see you. I told her what a large man you are in certain places."

Clara watched him relax.

"I see. Very kind of you."

She decided to play along, make the bastard pay for the pain he'd caused others. She stepped forward, offering out her hand. "I'm Lady Hamilton of Grosvenor Square."

The priest stood up and took her hand.

"Will you get it out and show it to me, father?"

"Well, I.. Um... I'm not in th…"

"Father. My girlfriend and I have a bet between us. She says she can take any man down her throat and keep him there until he comes. I said you were too big for such. We're here to settle the bet."

"You wish to suck me off?" the priest asked.

"No, I wish to swallow you. My young muscles are strong. Yes, I'll gag, I always do, but I always keep it down until a man is drained and finished so not even a single drop is left inside him." She told him, licking her lips and then kissing the side of his face. She put her lips up close to his ear and whispered, "If you help me win my bet, I'll return on my own another night and see if I can take you in my arse."

She heard the sound of cloth being lifted and smiled at him as she knelt. His cock dangled there, and he was holding his priest frock up high. She licked it and waited for a response. It immediately stood to attention. She took it in her mouth, letting some of it slide down her throat before snapping her teeth together, coughing it up, and taking the gushing cock into her mouth again, sucking and drinking from the red fountain of life.

She never heard him scream, as he couldn't. Falcon had already taken his throat into his dog teeth, and after ripping it apart, was letting the geyser there flood into his stomach and his veins.

Veyl landed at his driver's house, slipped in, and went down to the cellar, undetected. The tunnel to the house, his home, was always left open. He made the journey and got to his lab, undetected. He sat in his favourite chair and poured himself a potion, not one he'd made himself; no… one of the finest that mortal man had ever made: whiskey.

He should avenge himself, he knew that. But now that they were all like him, bar Maggie and Eric, how?

It was late. Were they all in bed? Were they living a lovely, wealthy life, using all the wealth he had amassed over decades? Did it matter? He could simply amass it again. What did they know about a vampire's existence? They were like children—no idea of what it takes? Had they learnt yet that every life they feed upon, their victims' thoughts and their journeys merge with their own? Experiences and emotions that would haunt them, possibly send them mad.

Had they learnt their lesson? Vampires cannot be killed. They can't kill him, and he can't kill them. What to do? That is the question.

As Falcon and Clara flew over the rooftops on their way home,

Falcon mind spoke to her, 'I sense Veyl's presence'.

Clara did too. 'Somehow, impossibly, he's reformed. What do we do'? She mind-spoke back.

'We kill him again and make sure he can never come back'.

They landed at the house and went straight to the lab, where they sensed his presence. He was sitting at the table, drinking whisky.

"We meet again," Veyl said calmly. "I hold no hatred or vengeance in my dead heart for what you all did."

"But we hate you, Veyl," Falcon told him.

"Yes, dear boy. I know you do."

"Why are you here?" Clara asked.

Veyl smiled. "Is this not my lovely home? You wish to live here, I think. Why not work like I did to get your own house?"

"This one came free," Falcon told him.

"Look," Veyl said. "The house is large, and with tunnels into all of London, it's easy to go out and feed. I suggest we all cohabit with a truce not to attack each other. I'll share more secrets with you and help you adjust and become stronger."

"We'll have to discuss it with the others," Clara said.

"Good. Can you do that, Falcon? I'd like Clara to stay and keep me company. I have been alone and missing being with others." Veyl said.

Falcon appeared reluctant to leave.

"Go on," Clara said. "He appears calm and genuine. I'll be fine."

Falcon nodded and left, but not before mind-saying, 'If he tries anything. Call out in my mind, and I'll come'.

"Please sit down, Clara," Veyl said.

Clara sat. Veyl filled another glass with whiskey and took it over to her. "Here. It's just whiskey, nothing else added."

She took it and tasted it. The heat from it felt good in her throat.

"Vampires can travel to the future and the past," Veyl said.

"What? How's that possible?"

He shrugged. "Maybe... possibly... reality is not actually real. I mean, look at us. How can we be dead and alive at the same time? It's completely against all scientific reasoning, but here we are—drinking whiskey together?"

Clara had often thought the same in the passing months. But he was crafty, sly. What was he looking for, something—baiting her with an intrigue?

"I can show you how to do it, if you like?" He said and sipped the whisky, looking at her intently.

"I know you, Veyl. You want something in return, don't you?"

He smiled. "Of course, but it's a fair exchange."

"Sex. Isn't it?"

"Huh. Last time we did that, I ended up in the sewers as dust, but I would love to experience that with you, Ruth, Annie, and Maggie, without those consequences. In return, I'll teach you all, everything I know and without malice."

"I can't speak for the others," Clara said.

He put his hands on her shoulders. It made her shiver. He noticed. "You think me evil, I know. But you now, and the others, except dear Maggie and Eric, are evil too in human eyes. It's because we're now all parasites, but consider human endeavour—the East India company, the newly formed banks, the crown... are they not all very sly, clever, parasites too?"

She had to agree in her head but said nothing to show she did.

"How do I know you're telling me the truth about time travel?"

He knelt in front of her, his face nearly on her lap, looking up at her. "Open your legs. Let me smell you, and in return, I'll demonstrate. Where do you wish to go, past or future?"

She wanted to see if it was true, but did she wish to pay the fare? Would she suddenly be in a fight to stop him harming her?

"I give you my word, Clara. No harm. I learnt my lesson. Just one little smell and I'll prove what I'm saying is true."

Clara slowly opened her legs and pulled her skirt up. "Go under, and I'll drop my dress down to form a tent. You can breathe in the air beneath, but nothing else. No touching."

He stooped forward and she threw her dress over him. She sat there looking up at a spider crawling across the ceiling, wondering to herself—who was walking into whose web. She intended to kill him, or at least make it so he could never form again. She had no doubt, that despite his words, he wanted the same for her and her new family. She could feel his hot breath against her vulva; a mixed sensation, to have him in an area of intimacy, like having a scorpion crawling along your thigh and perversely feeling sexually excited.

"Show me now. And if it's true, I'll have sex with you once you show me how to do it on my own." She said loudly.

His head came out. "How do I know you'll keep your word if I show you how to do it first?"

She looked down, closing her legs, "We can work that out, after you've proven it to be true."

"Mind-tell the others not to come down here first. I sense them moving down the hallways," he said. "And then, I will show you. Past or future, Clara?"

'Falcon', she mind-said, 'Don't come down. Wait until I beckon you, please'.

She looked down at Veyl. "Take me to two hundred years from now."

He stood up and said, "Best then, you cuddle into me and close your eyes until I teach you how to do it."

She hesitated.

"Trust me. I want willing sex, not me trying to take you by force. I'll earn it." He told her.

She was still uncertain, but she wanted to see. She stood up and put her arms around him, and he pulled her in tightly to her.

"Don't let go until I say so. I don't want you to be stuck in the future or spend months looking for you in a year between now and then if you let go too early."

She closed her eyes.

"Here we go. I don't like doing this. I once ended up in a war zone right as an artillery shell hit. It took me a week to pull myself back together." He told her.

There was a strange sensation, Clara felt, one like she had never experienced before. If she had to explain it to the others, she would be lost for words. It was like being weightless, but more—something of the mind; it was as though she never belonged anywhere, not in any era, or place. It passed.

"We're here," he said.

She opened her eyes. They were outside in an alley. There was noise everywhere, overwhelming her with its strangeness.

"We are in the wrong dress for this age," Veyl said. "But this alley is next to a theatre. Come, I'll take you to an ale house on the corner. They'll think we're theatre people. But first, wait here."

He flew up, leaving her standing there, bewildered and lost. She needed to wee, and moved back further into the shadows. Was this not like when she was lost, impoverished, and he found her?

She squatted, pulled her knickers down, and weed. There was a pleasure in weeing; she often wondered why. Was it the fact that since birth we are told in those first few years... nay, not told, *trained,* to go on command? Was the pleasure the fact of simply relaxing rather than spending life in tension?

Veyl returned to catch her still squatting and urinating. "My, what a pretty sight. It's lovely to see you practising my favourite perversion."

She stood, pulling her knickers up. "Where did you go?"

"To get money we can use in the ale house."

"How?"

"I fed as well," he replied.

"You robbed someone?"

"He had no further need of money. Come on. A pint of lager?" Veyl said.

Lager? A new word, she thought.

The ale house was like nothing she had ever seen. Lights glowed brightly with no sign of lamp oil or gas. How? And the women were half-dressed, with short dresses, tattoos, and so many of them, along with the men, so fat. Veyl was at the bar ordering drinks. A lot of people were gazing at them, presumably because of her and Veyl's attire.

A young man approached. He reached her table. "I guess it's good to have a drink after a show?"

She looked up, smiled, and nodded. "Yes."

He sat. "I'm Tom. I love the cinema more than the theatre. Mind you, period plays are very good."

"Yes. What work do you do?" She asked.

"Me? I work on building new housing estates. I have my own business, delivering and laying concrete."

"I see."

Tom whisked out a card and offered it to her. I saw you come in with another actor. Here's my card. Give me a call when you are not performing."

He got up and left as Veyl returned with two glasses of lager. She put the card in her pocket.

"What did he want?" He said as he sat.

"Sex, I think. Why is everyone covered with tattoos and look so fat? And what are those little boxes they keep holding and looking at?"

Veyl smiled. "Try the lager."

She sipped some and made a face. "It's all fizzy."

"Modern ale is like that. I quite like it myself. The little boxes you mention are called mobile phones. The people here talk to each other using them."

"How do they work?"

"All too much to explain. Another time. Drink up, Clara. This is just a brief visit to prove what I told you was true."

They drank together in silence. She studied everything and wondered. As she finished her drink, she saw a little black box sitting on a table near the door, and the people there, young and engaged, laughing. She wanted it.

"I'm ready to go," she told Veyl.

They stood and headed for the door, and as they passed the table with all the people laughing and chatting, with speed so fast to be seen by the eye, she stole the little black box and put it in her pocket.

They were back in Veyl's laboratory. Veyl smiled. "Time to keep your side of our little exchange."

"Yes, you took me to the future. Well done. But how do I do it?"

Falcon mind-whispered to her, 'Are you okay?'

'Yes. Don't come. I'm learning something that will help us. I'll come up later. All is good', she mind-said.

"What you do," Veyl started. "Is, you spread your wings and cover your body with them, then pick a time in your head, and say 'take me there', and it's as simple as that."

"Would you mind if I try it first to prove your statement is true?" She asked.

"Of course. But sex after, okay?"

"Yes. The secret is worth it."

She tried it and found herself back outside the ale house. She had an idea and went straight inside.

The Chair

Chapter 18: The Chair

Clara returned to find Veyl sitting and drinking whiskey. "I poured one for you. Where did you go on your test run?"

"Back to where we left, as I know I could do it safely."

"Satisfied? I poured that one for you," He said, pointing at a full glass.

She sat and sipped the whiskey. "You kept your end of the deal. I'll keep mine."

"Good. Finish your drink and then, please take off your clothes, and I'll tell you what to do."

She looked at him with suspicious eyes. "No pain or whipping me. Sex? Yes. But nothing more."

"Of course," he replied with a smile.

She finished the whiskey and removed her clothes. "What now?"

"Please get onto the chair," he told her.

"What? Your bloody torture device?"

"Yes, but not to hurt you. It has many uses. I promise you—no torture. You'll have a fantastic orgasm, trust me."

Clara had plans of her own. She wanted him dead. She would go along with it for the final plan in her head to work. She could always call on Falcon and the others with mind talk if he started to hurt her.

She went to the chair and sat in it. "The last time I sat in here, you caused me great pain."

"I know. I was teaching you what suffering is. Now I'm going to show you an infinite pleasure. Please allow me to strap you in. The chair will prepare you for bliss, which I will deliver."

He did up straps, and she calmly let him do them.

"There. I just need to operate a few levers, and I'll undress too. Comfortable?" He said.

He went behind the chair, and Clara heard gears meshing and turning, as the seat she was on, folded away—she sat on nothing but thin air, held to the back of the chair and her straps. Her feet were on two metal plates that slid apart as the straps around her upper thighs pulled her legs wide open.

The chair, what remained of it, tilted back at an angle until she was at a 45-degrees angle, her vulva gaping open.

He reappeared at the front and surveyed her, starting to undress. "Ah, a beautiful sight. I trust you are comfortable and not in any pain?"

"I appear to be okay." She replied softly.

He came over to her, unfolding his wings and flapping them so he hovered up in front of her. She could see his blood-gorged penis standing so straight, one would think it had a bone of steel at its core.

"I see my gaping vulva has affected you, Veyl."

"Indeed, it has. I am going to show you how a vampire can fuck you without ever touching your body—like this."

He swooped down, angling himself so his cock drove into her vagina with such force it took her by surprise and filled her in that one movement, causing her vagina to flood with lubricants. She heard his wings flap in a kind of rhythm, and his body thrust in and completely out; in to the hilt, and out, over and over again.. It was extraordinary, she thought. Not once did their bodies touch, save the base of his cock pressing against her open vulva, where it disappeared into his torso.

It was exciting and sensual; she was brought to orgasm fast, and she shook and moaned in bliss. He didn't stop, but instead, increased his pace, ramming in and out of her, and then a new thing: his cock thrust into her anus and all the way up her rectum. It was out in a trice and all the way into her vulva. He moved with such speed and accuracy, it felt like two men were fucking her, one in each orifice. She liked it—nay, fucking loved it. She was rising already to another orgasm, and when it came, it rose through her body from deep in her bowels. It was powerful, so much so, she emptied her bladder, spraying a geyser with such ferocity and power that she could see the top of it as it broke to fall like warm rain down over her body. It amplified the intensity of the high, smashing into her brain and overwhelming it before the bliss came that took away all thought, and she merged with the spirits of all that once lived in reality, but were now joined in a cloud of love.

And still he pumped into her vagina and her rectum, but now it seemed like a third person had joined this use of her body, as she gagged as his wet cock slid into her mouth and all the way down into the depths of her throat. She marvelled, even as she choked, at his speed to fuck her so, in three places as though three men were really fucking her.

She heard him orgasm too, with sperm in her mouth and throat, and more pouring from her anus and vulva—but he still didn't stop. If anything, he went faster and faster before screaming out a long deep groan and collapsing onto her, his reptile wings fluttering to rest against her sides. He lifted his head and kissed her seed-pouring mouth with a gentleness that denied her understanding of him.

"That was truly beautiful. Thank you, Clara." He whispered.

He breathed slowly, shut his eyes and lay his head down onto her breasts. For a while, she thought him asleep, until she heard and felt his wings furl up and disappear into his back. He climbed off and went to the back of the chair. She heard gears turning and felt the chair restoring.

He returned to stand in front of her. "That was the best fuck I've ever experienced. How was it for you?"

"Dramatic and powerful," she told him.

He released the straps and offered his hand to help her stand.

She took it and said, "I want us to take the others forward in time tomorrow. Is that okay with you?"

"Sure. We'll go as a family, exploring the amazing future."

" I bid you goodnight, then," she said, picking up her clothes and leaving.

She got into bed with the others. Ruth giggled and said, "You smell of sperm and piss."

"Sorry," she said. "There was a price to pay to learn something incredible."

"Go on. Tell us, then," they all said together.

She did, explaining everything and sharing details of her plan.

"That's very risky," Falcon said when she finished.

"Yes," Clara said. "But do you all want to live with him?"

The consensus was a resounding no.

"So, we'll do it and be rid of him once and for all," Clara said, turning into Falcon, cuddling him tightly, as she fell asleep.

They had met Veyl at breakfast time. As they ate together, a discussion ensued about time-travel, which could only be done by vampires or by non-vampires if carried by one. It meant both Eric and Maggie would need the help of the others to go forward and backwards in time.

They had done it, with Maggie and Eric being carried between Ruth, Falcon, and Clara, but they were still in the air, flying, to a destination guided to them by Clara. Unbeknownst to Veyl, she had arranged a rendezvous with Tom, the man who had spoken to her in the ale house.

"There it is," Clara said, pointing down. "The way they build houses in this age."

They looked to see a vast swathe of the countryside with hundreds of houses sitting on concrete. Huge machines levelled the ground or poured concrete, and hundreds of workers were spread out amongst the buildings, working like ants. They landed under Clara's instructions at the entrance to what looked like a temporary office—metal, with a sign above the door, which said, 'Tom's Concrete Ltd'.

"Wait here while I see if my newfound friend is inside," Clara told them, checking all wings were safely put away.

She came out a few minutes later, with a man beside her. "Tom, these are actors from our play. We got a carriage…"

"Taxi," Veyl interrupted. "A taxi from London, sharing the expense, you understand."

"Yes. We're all fascinated to learn about house building and how concrete is used." Clara finished. And then introduced everyone by name.

"I see," Tom said, looking up at them and their strange garments. "You all look very authentic. Victorian or Georgian?"

"King George's reign," Veyl answered.

"Good. You wish to see the whole process, then, Clara tells me?"

"Yes, right from how concrete is made to the laying of it," Ruth said.

Tom looked at her and thought she looked prettier than even Clara and Maggie.

"I'll show you, but in return, each of you lovely ladies must give me a Georgian kiss," Tom said, smiling.

"We'll gladly smother you with kisses," Ruth said. "And if you show us well, I'll treat you to a Ruth special."

"Really, what's that?" He asked.

Ruth sidled up to him, her lips brushing his ear as she whispered, "A fuck together on your desk in there." She pointed.

He stared at her, eyes wide. "Now, that would be a real treat. Okay. Wait here a moment, I'll get you some hard hats. It's a site safety rule."

"Here we are then. Most concreters use another process. They have the mix already delivered. and they add water and bring the slurry here in special lorries. I don't do that. I crush the limestone rocks on site, mix the powder with sand and aggregate, add water, mix it well and lay it where required. I'm about to make a batch to put down on a playground over there," Tom said, and pointed.

"Can we actually see the rocks being turned into powder?" Clara asked. It was the most important part of her plan."

"Yes, but be careful to stay on the gantry. We don't want any accidents. Follow me."

They followed Tom up a ladder and along a gantry until they were over a large cylindrical metal container.

"If you look down, the final limestone rocks are going in. There. It's done. The grinders and pulverisers will start after the lid closes," Tom told them.

'Ruth, distract Tom. I need to act while the lid is still open', Clara mind-said.

"Tom, I think some grit has gone into my eye," Ruth said. "Can you look for me" She offered him a hankie. "See if you can wipe my eye carefully."

Tom was next to her immediately. She pulled back the lid of her right eye as he took the hankie. Clara checked that Tom wasn't looking, and turned to Veyl. "Look at the process. Isn't it incredible compared to our time?"

She pointed at the slurry. He leant over the gantry to take a look, and she timed it perfectly, moving with super-human speed to grab his legs at the ankles—yanking them backwards so he toppled over and fell.

She watched as he tried to get his wings open, but was too surprised and bewildered to do it before he fell into the slurry and the lid closed fully.

"I can't visually see anything, but if you keep still, I'll give it a gentle wipe," Tom said.

Annie came up to Clara. "Veyl fell."

"Ssshh, Annie. We'll pretend he went back down to the ground."

Annie's eyes took on the gaze of someone looking inward and thinking. "Ah, yes. I see." She winked.

The machine below started to make a deafening sound. Clara thought of the monster within, as blades of steel cut his body to pieces.

"All done. Any better?" Tom asked Ruth.

She blinked and feigned relief. With a beaming smile of gratitude, she said, "Yes. Brilliant. You are a prince for doing that." And she kissed him gently. "Thank you, Tom."

He turned to Clara. "We'd best go down. The grinders will start any moment, and we'll be deafened by the noise they make. Oh, where's the man... um... Veyl?"

"He got bored and left. Said he'd meet us at the road when the taxi comes." She pulled out the little black box she'd stolen to show him. "I'm to call them when we're nearly ready to go."

"Follow me, and I'll take you to where that batch of concrete is laid and levelled," Tom told her.

A lorry pulled up.

"Half the concrete will be laid here and half will be sent to a smaller site a mile away," Tom told them, pointing. He had taken them to where a school was being built. This dries very fast and will be hard enough to walk on in an hour. By tomorrow morning, it will be so solid and thick that only the most powerful machines would ever shift it or break it up again."

Clara watched with dark fascination as the flexible pipe pumped the grey, semi-liquid concrete out, and men stroked and levelled it with hand tools. Veyl was in there, in that flowing mass, and in an hour, the sum of his parts would be forever separated, locked into the concrete.

"Fantastic," Clara said. "I think we've seen enough. We have a performance shortly, so we'd best leave soon."

"I need to fulfil my promise to Tom," Ruth said

"Of course. We'll wait outside the office for you," Clara said, and in her head, mind-added, 'Don't you dare feed on him'.

They waited outside listening to the body movements within, until Ruth came out looking fresh and smiling. "Right. Shall we be off then?"

"Yes," Clara said. "A good day and a safer future together. The monster will never bother us again."

end

www.ingramcontent.com/pod-product-compliance
Lightning Source LLC
Chambersburg PA
CBHW050837180626
46814CB00007B/2494